Crave

By Cathy Yardley

CRAVE

Crave

Cathy Yardley

red

AVON

An Imprint of HarperCollins*Publishers*

HarperCollins books may be purchased for educational, business, or sales promotional use. For information please write: Special Markets Department, HarperCollins Publishers, 10 East 53rd Street, New York, NY 10022.

FIRST EDITION

Designed by Diahann Sturge

Library of Congress Cataloging-in-Publication Data
Yardley, Cathy.
  Crave: the seduction of Snow White / Cathy Yardley.—1st ed.
    p. cm.
  ISBN 978-0-06-137607-8
1. Fairy tales—Adaptations.   I. Snow White and the seven dwarfs. English.
II. Title.
  PS3625.A735C73   2008
  813'.6—dc22   2007043362

08 09 10 11 12   OV/RRD   10 9 8 7 6 5 4 3 2 1

To my husband, Joe . . .
because they all are, with damned good reason.

Acknowledgments

I'd like to thank my agent, Annelise Robey, and the team at Jane Rotrosen, for being so incredibly supportive. It's been a long haul, and I appreciate your patience.

Also, I'd like to thank my editor, Erika Tsang, for believing in the fairy tale concept that I've been developing for five years.

Chapter One

"Why won't you simply die?"

Beth woke with a scream, her heart pounding heavily in her chest and the image of cruel, icy blue eyes following her from the dream. She forced herself to breathe, slow, measured breaths. A full moon illuminated her small room and she took comfort in the familiar surroundings: the clothes she'd neatly folded on her ladder-back chair, the handmade stationery neatly stacked on her small writing table, the colorful quilt she'd sewn herself, folded on her small wooden chest at the foot of her bed. The window threw an oblong square of moon-light on the smooth plank floor, showing her hand-braided rag rug. Everything was as it should be. It even smelled homey and familiar, like oatmeal soap and lavender.

It was all right. She was all right. Her heartbeat resumed its natural rhythm.

She was on the Compound, and everything was exactly as it should be.

She stood up on shaking legs, making her way toward the large open window and breathing in the summer night air, thick with humidity and heat. She hugged herself, shivering despite the temperature. Judging from the position of the moon, she'd say it was some time after midnight, maybe even closer to one or two in the morning.

Hiking up the hem of her long-sleeved nightgown, she stepped over the window ledge, putting a bare foot out on the soft grass. She hadn't had the nightmare in years, but she knew that dread usually followed in its wake. She did not want to be confined in her room when the claustrophobic feeling of fear struck.

She walked toward the woods, glancing at the darkened buildings around her. The women's dormitory was pitch-black, with most of the windows not only shut but shuttered, despite the heat. The men's dormitory across the Commons was a mirror image. The Dining Hall was completely still: it wouldn't be used for hours. The burnished metal Bell of Hours hung by the raised dais in the middle of the Commons, mute and glinting dull and ponderous in the moonlight. Even the stately Founders' House was dark and silent. She pushed past all of it to the nearby woods, looking around cautiously as she took hasty, quiet steps.

Once she was enveloped by the dark shadows of the trees, she breathed a little easier, feeling some of the tension retreat from between her shoulder blades. A little zing of excitement shot through her, something she'd forgotten. It had been a long time since she'd sneaked out of her room at night for a forest stroll. She tried so hard to obey all the tenets of belief the Founders had laid down, since it seemed to her they asked so little, and she received so much in return. But this was such a little transgression, she felt sure that even the strict Founders might understand.

She had a secret, favorite place: a meadow, carpeted in downy soft grass, dotted with beautiful wildflowers in yellow and purple and blue. Nestled in the heart of the forest that the Compound's high barbed-wire fence encircled, the meadow was her sanctuary-within-a-sanctuary, a place she could be totally alone. And safe. She would sit on the soft grass, amidst the daisies and wild roses, and just smile at the sheer, simple pleasure of it all.

Her life revolved around small, simple pleasures.

She was just to the edge of the clearing when a male voice pierced the night air.

"There you are."

Beth froze. The fear she'd been gradually letting go of leaped forward in a wave, clenching her heart in a stranglehold.

Then, she heard a husky feminine laugh. "Here I am."

Beth's heart restarted with the force of a cannon. She hadn't been discovered, as she'd feared. The male voice wasn't even talking to her.

Cautiously, she hid behind a thick, gnarled oak, peering out into the moon-drenched field.

The couple was already in the meadow, standing in front of each other, laughing and speaking in low voices that Beth could still hear clearly.

"I can't believe you're here."

"I can't believe I'm here!"

The man leaned forward, running his fingers through her long hair. Then he brought her face close to his and they stood there for a long moment, the soft, moist sound of their kisses blending with the night sounds of nature.

Beth stared, unable to move, barely able to breathe. All thoughts of retreat vanished in a blink.

After a few minutes, the woman made a low moan of need, her hands rubbing along the man's arms, her fingers digging into his shoulders. She pressed closer to him, her body molding against his, and his moan was an echo of hers. Their kiss grew more insistent, hungrier. His hand slid down from her hair to her throat, then moved to cup one of her breasts. The woman broke apart from him, gasping. "Henry," she murmured, stroking his face.

Beth's mouth fell open. Goodman Henry? He was one of the younger male Penitents, perhaps in his late thirties. And she thought she recognized the woman's voice now as well. Goodmaid Lydia. Lydia had only been in the Compound for a year or so and mostly kept to herself. Beth didn't know her very well.

Apparently, Beth didn't really know her at all.

How long has this been going on? Beth wondered, peering intently, disbelief adding to her chaotic tumble of fear and anger and shock.

Henry sucked at Lydia's neck, and her fingers crept to the buttons on her nightgown, undoing them slowly, whether out of seduction or unsure fingers, Beth couldn't tell. Henry continued his slow savoring, even as he removed his hand from Lydia's breast long enough for her to open the gown, slipping it off one shoulder. Her skin glowed like fresh cream in the moonlight, her red hair leached of color, looking almost as black as Beth's own. Henry's hand moved back to Lydia's breast, covering it, squeezing it. Lydia slipped the other side of the gown off, letting the heavy garment slide to the flare of her hips. She wore no bra. Beth could see the naked curve of her back, the slight shadow of her buttocks emerging from the pooled nightgown. Henry let out a growl of approval as he kissed her shoulders, holding her tight.

Beth held her breath. She barely recognized the rough feel of bark beneath her fingertips, as she clung to the tree for stability, feeling suddenly dizzy.

Now Henry moved lower, his mouth going to where his hand had been, turning the two of them in the process. From this angle, Lydia's nipple was sharply outlined in the moonlight. Beth could see the slow lapping motion of Henry's tongue as he teased Lydia's areola, licking at the nipple itself, coaxing it with light, flicking motions until it pointed. Lydia's breathing sped up, and her fingers went to work on Henry's shirt, finally giving in to impatience and tugging at it. He laughed, an almost feral sound, and stopped what he was doing long enough to yank the shirt over his head, tossing it to the ground. All that was left was his pajama bottoms. Lydia slid her naked torso along his, and he closed his eyes, tilting his head back, his voice a low, unintelligible sound of torturous pleasure. His fingertips dug into Lydia's hips, raising them to meet the thrusting motion of his pelvis. Then, gently, he nudged her gown, letting it fall the rest of the way to the grass.

Lydia wore nothing underneath, Beth noticed immediately.

Her buttocks were full and curved, shaped like a teardrop. Lydia sighed as Henry's hands roamed over her sloped hips, flexing experimentally. "Your turn," she said, her whisper carrying to Beth's burning ears.

Lydia reached for the drawstring of his pants, undoing the knot slowly. Henry's face was drawn, like a man straining under a heavy load, as her fingers finally undid the fastener and she ran her fingers beneath the fabric. "Don't tease," he growled.

"Just taking my time," Lydia countered, her voice full of mischief. "But if you're in such a rush . . ."

With a quick motion, she stripped off his pants, and Beth stifled a gasp. She saw the jutting silhouette of his penis, pointing at Lydia. Beth bit her lip, her eyes widening. She couldn't make out details, but even this dark glimpse was more of a man than she'd ever seen in her life.

Her breasts suddenly felt heavy, her nipples throbbing with an almost painful ache. She barely registered the dampness growing between her legs.

Beth was only consciously aware of two things. First, that what she was watching was not only against the rules of the Penitents, but also one of their most severely punishable offenses. Beth ought to flee from being even tangentially related to the act that was occurring.

Her second thought, however, was that she could not force her body to move from the spot, nor stop from witnessing the sexual drama unfolding before her.

"I've wanted your cock all week," Lydia said.

"Has your pussy missed me?" Henry's hand disappeared

between Lydia's thighs. "Yes. Yes, I can see it has. It's nice and wet."

"Just for you," Lydia breathed. "Fuck me, Henry. I want to feel your rock-hard cock stroking against my clit, pounding into me."

"It drives me crazy when you talk like that," Henry responded. "I never even knew—"

His sentence was interrupted by a groan when Lydia knelt down in front of him. Her lips circled his erection and she lapped at him as if he were some delectable dessert. His hands bunched in fists by his thighs as she cupped his balls, taking him even deeper into her mouth. He rocked his body forward, pressing toward her in a hypnotic rhythm.

Beth rubbed her damp palms against her nightgown, inadvertently pushing the coarse fabric against her all-too-sensitive thighs. Her breathing was uneven. Her heart threatened to beat out of her chest.

Lydia stopped, leaning back against the soft grass. "Now," she said, her legs spread wide.

Henry needed no further encouragement. His erection bounced jauntily as he covered her, his hand moving between them, positioning his cock at her opening. They both moaned as he slid into her, his hips meshing with hers. His hand stayed between them, moving industriously.

Lydia's head rolled from side to side, her eyes closed, her mouth open in a wide "o" of pleasure. "Yes, oh, please . . ." she chanted, and her legs moved higher on his hips as he began to thrust into her with slow, measured motions.

He leaned forward, taking one of her breasts into his

mouth, never missing stride. Lydia cried out in obvious release, her legs wrapping around his waist and her pelvis bucked against him as he plunged into her.

Beth leaned against the tree, breathing as if she were running in a marathon. Her stomach was clenched in a hard ball. She pressed her thighs together tightly, trying to stop the throbbing that was building. Her breasts tingled, her nipples hard against her nightgown. Hormones that she'd thought she'd successfully forced into hibernation through years of hard labor and absence of temptation suddenly sprang to life.

Despite the fact she was a virgin, she wanted sex . . . hard, driving, consuming sex.

She shivered, clenching her teeth. The hunger was almost unbearable, and she pressed her shoulder against the bark, slouching like a drunkard, unable to keep her feet as the wash of desire hit her like a tidal wave.

Lydia was gyrating her hips, her breathing short and staccato as machine gun fire. "Deeper," she chanted. "I want to feel your cock all the way inside me."

Henry complied, lifting her legs until they were hooked over his shoulders. "You feel . . . so . . . damned good," he said, the muscles of his torso shifting and his buttocks clenching and unclenching as he plowed into her, his balls bouncing against her buttocks. "That's it, baby. Take me in."

Lydia shifted as well, her pelvis arching to meet his every thrust. His face grew harsh with concentration, and she was muttering incoherently, pinching and kneading her breasts as her hips moved wildly against him. His hips rocked forward and back, his hands holding her waist and pulling her to meet his every plunging motion.

"Harder!" Lydia cried out. "Oh, Henry, fuck me harder!"

Henry groaned, his hips slamming against her, the slapping sound of their flesh getting louder.

"More!"

Lydia moved her legs from his shoulders, back to his waist. She sat up, clutching at him. He pulled her, and she was straddling him, the two of them sitting face to face. Her legs wrapped around him, and it was as if she were trying to meld with him. They kissed fiercely, tongues mating as their hips bucked and twisted against each other, the sound of their moaning and panting speeding uncontrollably.

Beth's hand crept to the juncture of her thighs, barely brushing her clit where it stood at attention beneath her layers of clothing. It had been a long time since she'd gratified herself . . . since she'd felt the need to. She watched as Lydia and Henry mated like wild animals, clawing at each other, their hips like pistons against each other as they sought their fulfillment. The sound of their frenzied sex only fueled Beth's need.

Lydia screamed out, a rippling cry. Soon after, Henry responded with a thick groan of triumph. Beth breathed heavily, tension and frustration lashing her like a whip. She bit the back of her wrist, the pain blotting out some of the need.

Lydia and Henry stayed joined for a long time, their breathing harsh and loud. Then Lydia stilled. "Did you hear something?"

Beth forced herself to hold her breath, keeping as still as the tree she was propped up against.

Henry was motionless, like a rabbit sensing a hawk. Then he shook his head. "Probably nothing," he said, but his voice sounded unconvinced. "Still . . . I guess we ought to be getting back."

"Already? I don't know that I'm done with you tonight."

"It's dangerous," Henry reminded her.

"That's part of the fun."

Henry's heavy sigh filled the meadow. "Once is enough for now."

Lydia stood up, her weight heavy on one hip, her arms folded. "Are you sorry I asked you to join me?"

"No, of course not," he said, but he was quickly slipping his pants on. "I'm just being careful."

There was a moment of silence.

"You know," Lydia commented, "you're not the only one that can satisfy me."

Henry stopped in the act of tying his drawstring. "I can only imagine you've found other men in this Compound to . . . *fuck*."

Beth inhaled sharply, surprised by the sharpness of their exchange, especially after what should have been a tender, heartfelt act.

Lydia laughed her husky laugh. "What makes you think it's a man?"

Henry frowned, puzzled. "You mean . . . wait. What do you mean?"

"You were sheltered even before you joined this group, weren't you?" Lydia's voice sounded both condescending and yet fond. "I mean a woman, Henry. I've definitely found pleasure with another woman."

"A . . . *woman* . . ." Henry's voice made the word sound foreign.

If Beth had been shocked by the goings-on in her meadow, now she was positively floored.

Lydia chuckled, reaching out to stroke the diminishing bulge in Henry's pants. "Can't you imagine," she purred. "Another woman, her breasts stroking against mine . . . her tongue delving deep into my pussy . . . her clit sliding along mine?" Her voice went breathless just describing it, and her eyes went low lidded.

"You wouldn't find anyone here," Henry protested, but Beth could tell he had already pictured the scenario in his mind. His cock, which had been slowly going flaccid, suddenly started showing signs of life.

"I already have," Lydia said.

"Who?"

"Never mind. If things work out, maybe you'll meet her." She released his drawstring. "Maybe more than meet her, if you can make it worth my while."

"You're wicked." Henry sounded admiring . . . and a little frightened.

"I know." To Beth's surprise, Lydia actually sounded a little saddened by that. "But as long as we're careful, we can have whatever we want."

She pushed his pants down, stroking his cock back to life. Then she tugged him back down to the ground, rolling him onto his back before straddling his newly engorged penis, sighing with pleasure as she slid over him. She started riding him with deliberate motions, her hips circling ever so slightly. He groaned with pleasure.

Get out of here.

Beth waited until the couple was well and truly occupied

with their own pleasure, the sounds of their sex covering the muffled steps of Beth's careful escape. She made her way back to the women's dormitory quickly, her heart still trip-hammering in her chest. She climbed back into her windows, closing her shutters and barring them.

It wasn't like she didn't know about sex. After ten years in her stepmother's palace, she had seen acts of depravity much worse, in the ballrooms, private chambers, even the very hallways. But despite that exposure, her body had never actually felt the pressure of a man's penis, pressing into her hungry flesh, filling her. Fulfilling her. She had come close to the sensation once, with one of the Queen's guards—a stolen moment that had ended in tragedy, when the Queen herself stepped in on the passionate interlude.

In the darkness, Beth huddled on her bed, hugging her knees to her chest.

In the ten years since she had joined the Penitents, she had willingly, even eagerly, embraced their tenets of abstinence and strict gender separation. She had buried her needs in the physical demands of their agricultural life: churning, weaving, washing, cooking. She made herself an exemplary Penitent, never giving them reason to question her . . . or her past.

But now, witnessing one stolen moment, it felt like floodgates had burst somewhere inside her. She realized that all of her physical labor had been in an attempt to ignore the inevitable burning desire that always simmered just under the surface. As long as she could pretend that sex didn't exist, she could barely hold on to the illusion she'd crafted for herself. But now, confronted with it so visually, the longings she'd locked up refused to be ignored. She wasn't sure what it would take to dam up the flood of needs that she'd been keeping at bay for ten long years.

Worse, she didn't know what might happen if she found someone who called to her unspoken hunger before she could get it back under control.

Chapter Two

Stephen Trent sat in the dining hall of the Compound, wondering what the hell he was doing there, or, more important, how the hell he was going to get out.

I'm going to kill Randall when I get back to the office.

Randall was his editor, and, generally, a damned good one. However, he had no idea what dope the man was smoking to consider this bunch of yahoos a dangerous cult, one worthy of his best reporter's time. Personally, Stephen suspected that Randall was punishing him for the bills he racked up on his last assignment. Infiltrating a jet-setting millionaire's fight club in Manhattan did not come cheap, and Stephen had spent a bundle on clothes, booze, strippers, and travel, just to fit in. He'd maxed out his expense account, and Randall had burst a blood vessel.

Stephen wasn't going to be spending a dime here, since one

of the tenets of belief was no real property. Stephen didn't even have his wallet. He felt naked without it. Which was a neat trick, considering the heavy, long-sleeved, high-collared clothes and hat he was being forced to wear.

He took a deep breath, inhaling the rich aromas of the plate of food in front of him. Ham steaks in a savory gravy, fluffy mashed potatoes, broccoli and cauliflower with some kind of cheese sauce. Light-as-air yeast rolls, slathered in butter. Some kind of custard pudding, crusted with brown sugar.

You might not be able to have sex in this joint, but apparently there was no sin in cholesterol. He bit into a roll, sighing with pleasure. *And let me say* amen *to that.*

As he tucked into his savory fare, he glanced up at the platform in the front of the dining hall. A broad table stretched out on it, and seated there were the seven Founders, the old guys who thought up this cozy little corner of abstinence. All dressed in black, they looked like Amish versions of Johnny Cash. They took themselves very seriously, he noticed. Too bad Stephen was having a hard time doing the same.

He'd only gotten there this morning, but from what he could see, the place was like a Quaker theme park. Everyone was pleasant, smiling, calling each other the archaic "Goodman" or "Goodmaid." Although, technically, Goodmen weren't supposed to speak to Goodmaids ever, or so he was instructed during orientation. Right now, he was sitting on the right side of the building, with the rest of the men, while the women were seated on the left side. The men got their food first; the women did all the cooking and serving. Apparently, they did all the cleaning, too. Women were also not allowed to leave the Compound, ever, for any reason, and certainly were prohibited from having any contact with outsiders, especially men. On the other side of the coin, the Penitent Goodmen had to leave the Compound, and work in the mines during the day, turning over their paychecks to the Founders. Traditional gender roles took on a whole new meaning here. Men brought home the bacon, women cooked it, and any talk of househusband or working woman was heresy. Still, nobody seemed to mind.

In fact, they were so cheerful, Stephen was starting to wonder if maybe the seven Founders weren't tossing Prozac in with the well water.

He grimaced in frustration, cleaning his plate and going for the custard. He figured he'd kill a couple of weeks here, gain a couple of pounds, and see if he could cobble together something about the quaint little throwback community that valued hard work with a cheerful smile over the evils of the city. It'd be a snore, but at least it would get him out of here.

One of the Founders stood up.

"I am Founder Amos," the man said, pushing his wire-rimmed glasses up on his bulbous nose. "I'd like to open by welcoming our newcomers to the Penitents. You have made the choice to join us, and stand apart from the temptations and downfalls of the world outside. . . ."

Stephen tuned him out, already familiar with the basic tenets: no sex, no drink, no drugs, no excess, lots of physical work. Follow the rules or else, yadda, yadda, yadda. Despite Amos's mild tone and even milder exterior, Stephen did have to give the guy credit for having a compelling speaking voice. Obviously, he was the leader, the brains of the organization. Stephen did a quick visual perusal of the rest of the crew. The only other one that stood out was a menacing guy on the end, Founder Robert. Robert had been the one that greeted the busload of newcomers, including Stephen, when they'd first arrived. "Welcomed" would have been too warm a word for Robert's form of introduction. The guy looked like a cross between an Amish farmer and a dockyard enforcer, easily six foot two and pure stocky muscle. Robert had made it clear to Stephen and his fellow new recruits that breaking the tenets of faith would not be tolerated, and then sent over a chilling smile when he pointed out that he himself was in charge of doling out punishment.

If Amos was the brains, Robert was evidently the brawn.

Stephen found his gaze wandering over to the other side of the building, where the women were sitting. They were a study in drab, all wearing long-sleeved, high-necked button-up dresses, in shades running the gamut from gray to black. They wore wimple-styled veils, allowing not even a wisp of bang to show. Nobody wore makeup.

Obviously, with these obstacles, it'd be hard for a woman to look her best, Stephen realized. But the deep frowns that most of the women sported did not help matters. They were listening to Amos's speech as if he were revealing the secret of life. It was sad, really. Stephen was about to turn his attention back to the Founder's speech when he realized that not all the women were staring at Amos with rapt attention.

His gaze locked with a pair of violet blue eyes, staring right back at him from under a fringe of long ebony lashes.

It was like slipping and falling on a frozen lake: he felt numb, and he struggled to breathe, as if the wind had been knocked out of him.

She was the most beautiful woman he'd ever seen, and considering the paper's ever-growing coverage of starlets and celebutantes, he'd seen plenty, splashed across the pages of the newspaper. But initially, it wasn't even the beauty of her face that caught his attention. It was the way she looked at him. Part fear, part longing, part pure sexual heat. She looked at him like he was a tall, cool glass of water, and she was dying of thirst. His cock stiffened from the look in her eyes alone.

It took her a second to look away. When she did, he finally took in the rest of her appearance. Her face was a perfect porcelain oval, with impossibly high cheekbones, delicately arched eyebrows, and full lips that were red as crushed raspberries, looking twice as delicious. Her hair was hidden behind a charcoal gray veil, and she wore a muted brown dress that was obviously a bit baggy on her. Still, he could see the delicate line of her swanlike neck before it was hidden by her collar, and the curve of her chin was gently sculptured. She smoothed down her veil with her hands. Her fingers were long, "piano-playing hands," as his family would say. Even her innocent gesture was graceful.

Founder Amos's voice had become a dull, incoherent buzz. The drab environment seemed to gray out completely, leaving only her, in a circle of light.

She must have felt the intensity of his stare. Either that, or the desire he'd seen in her eyes compelled her to look back at him again. Her next look was fleeting, but packed a punch. Just as quickly as she'd glanced, she looked away, and he saw the point of her pink tongue lick her full lower lip nervously.

His body went completely hard in a rush, all his muscles

tightening, his heart rate increasing like a train picking up momentum.

Who the hell is this woman, and how is she doing this to me? He hadn't felt this quickly out of control ever, not even as a teen. This was unprecedented.

No woman had ever given him a raging hard-on just from *looking* at him, for Christ's sake.

He wanted to stand up, walk over to her. Ask her for her name. See if she wanted to have dinner sometime, maybe a drink or three. Check out his apartment . . . until breakfast. He'd never been so ham-handed when it came to finessing women, but then again, women hadn't complained. On the contrary, he'd had more lovers than he was necessarily proud to remember, and more times than not, they'd approached him.

But this woman wasn't hitting on him. She wasn't playing deliberately coy. She wasn't playing at all. It was the naked, raw emotion in her eyes that attracted him, he realized. In a line of work where his job was listening to lies and fighting for truth, he found her clear and honest reaction not only rare, but intoxicating. He could be wrong, of course. She could be one of the world's best undiscovered actresses. But as a reporter, he trusted his instincts, and as a man, he trusted his body. Both knew that the woman was genuine.

His instincts trusted her.

His body wanted her.

"I cannot stress this enough. *No male and female interactions of any sort are permitted in the Compound.*" Founder Amos's voice shifted from gentle to reprimanding, from camp leader to parole officer. The change was dramatic, and startling. Stephen pried his gaze from the blue-eyed woman long enough to see Amos glaring at him specifically. Stephen winced: he was busted. By the top dog, no less.

When was the last time a woman had managed to distract him from his work?

Easy enough to answer. Women *never* distracted him from his work. After all these years, he'd gained more satisfaction from his articles than from his affairs.

"There are certain specific interactions that are obviously taboo," Amos continued, his face pruning up at even the tangential reference to sex. "But beyond . . . *that*, there is strict gender segregation here. Men and women do not eat together, work together, or converse in any prolonged manner. Side by side, we live, but we maintain constant vigilance."

Stephen fought to stay focused, but his wayward eyes kept wanting to look back, see if she were still staring at him. He wanted to study her face. There was something about her. Something captivating. Something magical.

His eyes narrowed abruptly.

Something familiar.

Chapter Three

Beth was breathing hard by the time she'd made it back to her darkened room. She shut the door, putting a hand on her heart, feeling the pulsing beat beneath her palm pounding out a fierce rhythm.

Who was that man?

She closed her eyes, picturing his face like it was burned on her memory. Mussed dirty-blond hair. His face looked chiseled out of marble, harsh planes and hard angles. But he didn't look like most of the other men that joined the Penitent compound. Most of the Newcomers who showed up were older, their faces permanently creased with bitterness, anger, and guilt. Some had looked at her with desire before, but it was always mixed in with a chaotic blend of embarrassment and disgust. In him, she'd seen none of that. His eyes were a deep, smoky greenish gray, like moss, and his lips were full and sensual in a purely masculine sense. He was ruggedly handsome, and although he was obviously strong, she sensed something lighter in him. The way he'd bitten into his dinner roll and smiled . . . she'd forgotten all about her own food when she saw the small ghost of a smile, the way he'd closed his eyes. He could just as easily be angry, she sensed, but he was obviously capable of happiness, lightness, a sense of humor.

She didn't realize just how appealing that trait could be in a man.

Beyond his face, she could tell that his body was impressive. He stretched out the cotton of his Oxford shirt with the telltale yoke of muscles that suggested broad, muscular shoulders. His hands looked strong, capable.

She swallowed hard, just thinking about his hands.

She paced around her small room in her bare feet, spasmodically clasping her hands in fists by her side. Her body felt like it was on fire.

She didn't even know his name, but it didn't matter. She wanted his touch, more than she'd wanted anything in a long, long time.

She considered going for another walk, but it was too early. Someone might see her. Besides, the way her luck was going, she might run into Henry and Lydia again—and her already hair-trigger system did not need another sensual slap. If she didn't get some kind of release, she thought she'd go mad.

She took off her day dress, standing in just her white cotton bra and panties. She was about to pull on her nightgown when she realized she was all alone in her room. No one else would come in.

There was a way she could get some relief.

She took a deep breath, then took off her bra and panties, feeling the still, hot air of her room on her naked skin. It felt lurid, but at the same time, her excitement increased slightly. She put her chair under the doorknob, jamming her door shut, just in case there was a bed check. Then she climbed on top of her covers, stretching out on her bed.

Technically, the Penitents frowned on any sort of sexual activity . . . even if there was only one participant. Self-gratification was a lack of self-control. She didn't indulge often, especially since she was usually able to wear herself out with the sheer physical labor of her daily chores. But tonight was an exception.

She shook her hair across the pillow, feeling its silkiness creep along her flesh. It hung beneath her waist by this point, but she normally had it pinned up and out of the way. Now, she luxuriated in the silky feel of it, cool against her hot skin. She stroked her hands down her neck, slowly stroking her breasts, circling them slightly. Abruptly, she thought of the man's hands, and she closed her eyes, imagining he was touching her. She shifted her direction, her palms cupping her breasts, her thumbs stroking along the sensitive bumpy skin of her nipples. She felt a flare of heat shoot through her, from her areolae straight down to the juncture of her thighs. Her breathing hitched slightly.

She wanted him. She wanted to feel him.

One hand continued to work at her breast, while her right hand smoothed down the plane of her stomach, feeling her pubic curls twining around her fingers. She stroked down the damp slot, parting the thick outer folds of skin until she reached the delicate inner petals of her vulva. Her clitoris was a semi-erect bump. She stroked it gently, placing a finger to either side of it and twiddling it with gradually increasing pressure. The bump hardened, and breathing started to turn into panting. Her hips raised off the bed, her pelvis tilting upward slightly as her thighs parted to give her hand better access. Her legs tensed.

It wasn't enough.

Her left hand released her breast to shift lower, and she sat up a little to accommodate the awkward angle. As her right hand continued to industriously work the nubbin of pleasure, causing tremors of sexual excitement to shiver through her system, her left hand reached lower, dipping past the clitoris, parting the inner lips to get to her vagina. She penetrated it slowly, pressing first one finger, then a second inside. Wetness washed over her fingertips, lubricating her entry, and she pressed deeper, stroking her fingers over the rough-wavy muscles that clenched and shifted beneath her touch.

She wanted it to be him.

She imagined how it might feel: the man's broad, naked body, here in the room with her. His broad hips shifting between her thighs, his hard, jutting cock parting her wet flesh. She bit her lips as her body started to respond to the fantasy. She imagined his blunt cock head, wet with her moisture, pressing inside her tight opening, stretching her, going deeper until it stroked against her secret spot.

She pressed her fingers in as deep as they would go, her wrist bending, sitting upright as she worked quickly, the pressure building. Her right hand was almost ready to cramp, but she kept working furiously, the waves of pleasure radiating from her clit making her hips jerk and pivot with desperate, clawing need. Her left hand kept thrusting, adding a third finger, spreading her . . . filling her.

He'd plunge into her, his thick shaft rubbing against her clit, the heft of him slamming into her as his body crushed her into the bed. Her breath came in gasping gulps, and her nipples were tight and hard. She threw her head back, the beginning ripples of release clutching at her. Suddenly, her fingers hit the right spot, high up on the inside of her, and she let out a cry as the orgasm hit her. She felt her fingers get coated with the sweet-sticky honey of her climax, and the way her pussy clutched at her hand tightly, shuddering against her. She stilled her left hand, while her right hand kept stroking her clit, drawing the release out, creating the aftershocks of pleasure that kept her shaking on her coverlet.

When it was over, she withdrew her hands, wiping them carefully on her towel. The room was stuffy, and smelled of her sex. She opened the window, naked in the darkness. The night air felt cool on her feverish skin.

For a second, she felt a blessed sense of relief, as the driving need backed off. Without the driving hunger for sexual release, she felt her mind slow, then steady.

What she felt then wasn't what she was ready for.

She felt . . . empty.

She closed her eyes in frustration. She *liked* her life on the Compound. She had plenty of women friends to talk to. She enjoyed the beautiful grounds, the tall trees, the flowers. The work was hard, but it was also fulfilling. The place was idyllic. While there were strictures, there was nothing she couldn't live with: no television, no radio. No sex. All that, added with the fact that this was the one place on earth she felt that her anonymity was safely preserved, giving those things up was a small price to pay to live in this agricultural Shangri-La.

But she hadn't realized, until she saw the man, that she could crave a totally different kind of company than her circle of women friends. How long had she been in here? Since she was seventeen . . . ten long years ago. In all that time, she'd only dreamed of one man's touch.

And that man was now dead, for touching her.

She walked back to her chair, pulling on her bra and panties with heavy limbs.

Until she'd stumbled across Henry and Lydia's forbidden tryst in the meadow, she hadn't known that she was hungry for more than the Compound's ample food stores. Now she knew that her body craved sex, despite her diligent efforts to tamp down the desire.

Until she'd seen the stranger, with his green eyes and small smile, she hadn't known she wanted a man's touch. No, not any man. *Him.* She didn't know that she could react that strongly to anyone, and here he was, temptation, come right to her doorstep. He might make living in her sanctuary unbearable.

She closed her eyes as she pulled on her nightgown.

Or he could make my life here complete if I acted like Lydia.

She pounded her pillow, climbing back into bed even though she knew sleep would be a long time coming. Lydia would be distressed if she was banished from the Compound, but she had lived on the outside world. Beth could not afford a tryst: the price was way too high. If she were banished, she would be thrown out into a world that would find out about her past, and seriously jeopardize her future.

Especially once people realized that she wasn't dead, as she'd so painstakingly made them believe, ten long years ago.

For an investigative reporter, Stephen was having one hell of a time finding the woman he'd seen at dinner the night before. For Christ's sake, the Penitent camp was just a couple of square miles in rural Pennsylvania. In a compound that was fenced in with barbed wire, no less. And the grand total population of this place was, what, maybe four hundred, with about half of them being women? Not to mention that the woman he was specifically seeking was breathtaking, beautiful enough to put the world's supermodels to shame. So really, how hard could it be to find her?

Very hard, apparently.

Stephen sighed. In his defense, the whole gender-separation thing was a pain in the ass. He couldn't go right over to where the women were sitting during meals and scout her out. He couldn't go into the kitchen where they worked, since domestic chores of any sort were designated a "Goodmaid's province." Another hurdle was the shapeless, drab clothes that all the women wore. If she had her back to him, she'd blend right in.

He grinned wryly. His editor had sold him on the angle that most of the people who joined the Penitents looked at it as a sort of Foreign Legion—a place to bury their pasts. If the woman was looking for a place to disappear, she'd picked a real winner.

Out in the few acres of fields, men were working . . . planting stuff, weeding stuff, something farmy. Stephen knew that he was supposed to be out there, too, but he was convinced that finding the woman was more important. He had talked to a few of his dorm mates, that morning during breakfast, but he didn't think there was a story there. They all gave him the same runaround: they just wanted to live pure lives, they were sick of the temptations and lack of morals on the outside, the whole nine yards. No, if he were going to make a story out of this, it'd be the throwback treatment of women here.

And if he'd decided on who he wanted to interview . . . well, so what?

He spotted a group of women trooping across the Commons, heading for the woods, baskets of laundry in their arms. And there, right in the middle of them, was his blue-eyed girl.

Gotcha.

His pulse picked up. He told himself it was because the sooner he could talk to the girl, the sooner he could get his story angle, and the sooner he could get out of this Amish ashram. But he knew that it had nothing to do with his story, and everything to do with seeing her again.

She was wearing another plain outfit, this time a lighter brown, resembling the cinnamon-apple oatmeal he'd eaten at breakfast. She wore a gray veil and carried her laundry basket tucked under her arm, balanced against her hip like a pro. He wondered how long she'd been here, to be so proficient. She didn't look old at all, maybe young twenties, if he had to guess. Other women were making their way with baskets, so he kept carefully back. No other men were following, he noticed. Good. Fewer potential witnesses.

He had every intention of breaking the "no gender inter-action" rule. He just hoped that the blue-eyed girl's obvious curiosity in him outweighed her loyalty to the cult's strict tenets.

He moved carefully, at a distance, so as not to alert his quarry. There was a shallow river snaking through the property—more like a big stream. The women spread out along its curving length, each staking out her own private clothes-washing turf. They didn't laugh, or sing, or even speak, as he would've expected them to. Instead, they worked in meditative silence. Absently, he remembered one of the tenets that Robert had been pushing on his opening-day intro.

Work hard, keep solitary, stay pure.

The blue-eyed girl moved off farther from the rest, going to a secluded nook where heavy foliage shaded a burbling section of water. Stephen moved into the shadows, watching her.

She sighed, glancing around. Then she tucked her veil up, revealing a swath of neck. Unbuttoning her sleeves, she rolled them up past her elbows, revealing the pale flesh of her arms. Her limbs were lithe, toned from hard work but not bulky with muscle. He watched as she quickly peeled off her shoes and socks, tying her long skirt in a knot to keep the edge from dipping into the rushing water. She stepped in, letting out a small gasp at the obviously cool water. Then Stephen heard her sigh with sensual pleasure, just standing there, her eyes closed, face turned toward the sun.

His cock tightened, going hard in a rush as he took in the tiny sound, the small, innocent look.

He cursed himself. It had been a while since he'd gotten laid, admittedly, but he'd gone for longer without his body being this damned unruly about it. He stared at her shapely calves, the delicate curve of her feet. It wasn't like she'd gotten naked. For that matter, he'd managed to stay unmoved at some women who had stripped down to pure skin.

Why the hell is she affecting me this way?

It wasn't like he was looking for a future with this strange woman, or anything. Hell, he probably had no shot at even a fling with the girl. He was just here to write a story—in, out, *wham-bam.* And unless he wanted to become like Abelard, living a monklike existence next to his ladylove the nun, then he'd better snap out of this weird schoolboy obsession and get his eye back on the brass fucking ring pretty quick. She might be beautiful, and mesmerizing, but in the end, she is just part of the story.

He stepped forward, clearing his throat.

She froze in the act of dipping a shirt in the water. Her violet blue eyes went wide, and her nostrils flared slightly. She didn't look like she was going to run, but at the same time, she didn't exactly look inviting. The hungry look she'd sent him the night before was clearly absent.

He smiled easily, stopping, giving her time to get used to him. "Hello," he said, making his voice sound as gentle and harmless as possible. He didn't want her suspecting anything.

Want some candy, little girl?

She didn't respond. Her breathing was shallow, and from

his closer vantage point, he could see her pulse beating strong and quick in the column of her throat.

He wondered what it'd be like to press a kiss against that trembling flesh.

He shook his head. *Focus, schmuck.* He needed to get her to relax, not bolt. He needed to gain her confidence. "So, ah . . . what are you doing there?" he asked carefully, blandly inquisitive, as if he were a documentarian.

Her expression changed. Her eyes narrowed, and she looked at him, then down at the shirt in her hand, the soap in the other. Then she looked back at him, and to his surprise, the tiniest quirk of a smile kissed her full lips. "I'm planting corn," she replied, a rich laugh in her voice.

Huh? "Planting . . . ?" He frowned a minute, baffled. Then he realized she was making fun of him. He grinned back broadly. "Duh. I guess it *is* pretty obvious what you're doing. What I meant was, why in the stream? Isn't there a washing machine here somewhere?"

She shook her head. "Machines are for people who want to waste their time on frivolities," she said, in a rote, wooden voice that suggested she was quoting one of the Founders. Which she probably was. "You shouldn't be here. You'll get in trouble."

The fear hadn't completely left her eyes, he noticed. She glanced around, as if the Founders were hiding behind a bush or something. But when she wasn't scouting, she was back to staring at him: quick, furtive glances, tracing over the entire length of his body. His skin tingled everywhere her gaze traveled.

Her skin flushed, a delicate, soft rose color.

"Well, it's my first day," he said casually. "I'm sure they'll cut me a break, right?"

She laughed softly. "You *are* new, obviously."

He liked the sound of her laugh. He smiled again, feeling warm. "I'm just trying to figure out how things work here." He paused, then held a hand out. "My name's Stephen, by the way."

She stared at his hand, then turned away from it, dredging the shirt in the water and scrubbing at it vigorously with soap.

"And you are . . . ?"

"B-beth." She rinsed the shirt clean, then threw it on the grass, picking up another and repeating the process.

"Beth. Goodmaid Beth." She didn't look like a Beth. She looked like something more evocative. Helen of Troy might work. "It's nice to meet you, Beth."

He took another step closer, and she didn't back away. She kept washing shirts, mechanically. He was almost in the water when she lifted a hand in warning. "Anything I can do to help?" he asked, waiting.

"I already told you, you're not supposed to be here." Her voice sounded breathless. "You'll get in trouble."

He shrugged.

"You're going to get *me* in trouble."

He took a step in the water. He was only two feet away from her. He could smell her—clean and soft, like some kind of summer flower. He couldn't think of the name, but he'd be able to remember this smell for the rest of his life.

"I'm not going to hurt you," he said. "I just want to know more about you."

He meant to say more about the Compound, the Penitents. But as soon as he got close to her, he knew he no longer gave a damn about those things—not right now. The article could wait. He wanted to know more about *her.*

"You can't," she said, her eyes darting toward the foliage.

"Why not?" He inched closer. Just a foot away, now.

"It's forbidden." Her voice was a low, lush whisper.

"Nobody can see us," he said. "Besides, we're just talking. There's no harm in that."

"Talking leads to liking," she said, her voice a high-pitched squeak as he took one more step forward. "Liking leads to . . . to lust."

"Another tenet of belief, huh?"

She nodded.

"And are you afraid of lust, Beth?"

He didn't know why he asked the question, but once it popped out of his mouth, he found himself riveted to her answer. He stared at her face, her lips, waiting for her next sentence.

Her indigo eyes turned suddenly haunted.

"Yes," she whispered. "Yes, I suppose I am."

He felt a cold chill in the pit of his stomach. Had she been abused? Was that what she was running away from? The thought nauseated him, filling him with both a pounding fury and an equally aching need to . . . what? Defend her? Protect her?

Save her?

He gritted his teeth, struggling to focus. "You don't have to be afraid of me," he said, trying to reassure her, even as his hands itched to free her from the ugly beige homespun she was shrouded in and cover her bare skin with his.

"Yes, I do," she countered.

His eyes widened. He was trying to be gentle, here. Was his body's intent that obvious?

"I promise, I won't . . ." He was about to say *I won't touch you*, but he found himself balking. "I won't do anything you don't want me to," he amended.

"I know," she said quietly. Her voice rang with sincerity . . . and trust.

He felt strangely humbled.

"Then what is there to be afraid of?" he said, striving for a light tone of voice.

She stared at him, and her tongue moved over her lips, a brief, catlike motion that she obviously didn't even know she'd done. The hunger in her eyes, her body, was palpable, and his body tensed in response. He was momentarily stunned by the sheer intensity of it.

"I want you to do things to me," she murmured. "That's why I'm afraid."

The moment the words were out of her mouth, she winced, appalled at her forwardness. She had no idea what possessed her to utter the words.

His eyes blazed, green and hot and smoky. She could smell the rich, masculine scent of him, like an expensive cologne. Momentarily, her senses went into overload. He was close enough to touch.

He was close enough to *taste*.

She closed her eyes, struggling to regain her sensibilities.

When she reopened her eyes, he was even closer to her.

"You affect me," he said, his voice husky. "It's the strangest thing. I've never felt anything like it."

She swallowed hard. "We shouldn't," she protested, but it was weak. She still made no move to go.

"I'm not doing anything," he said, and she knew that *yet* was unspoken, but definitely hanging tangibly in the air. "But . . . what do you want me to do to you, Beth?"

She could feel the heat of a blush crawl up her neck. She threw the wet shirt into the basket, grabbed another from the pile, scrubbing it with more force than was necessary. "We can't." It was meant to be a statement, possibly even an order. It came out sounding like a question. Almost a plea.

His hand covered hers, unbelievably warm compared to the chill of the water. She jerked her hand away—but only after a long second. Her breasts tightened and her chest compressed. She was having trouble breathing.

"Pretend you weren't here, in this place, with these rules," he said softly. "What would you want me to do?"

She closed her eyes, fighting to get some semblance of control back over her chaotic body. His scent flooded her nose. She breathed him in, and her vagina clenched like a fist.

"I don't know," she replied, frustration giving her words a jagged edge. "Something. Anything." She swallowed hard. "To . . . touch me."

He was silent. She opened her eyes, unsure of what she'd see in his face.

His hunger matched her own, if possible. But his expression was tender, and a little quizzical.

"Are you a virgin, Beth?"

The heat of her blush intensified. "I have to go," she mumbled, still not moving.

"A virgin," he marveled. "In this day and age."

"I've been here since I was seventeen." She didn't know why she felt compelled to justify the state of her sexual experience, or lack thereof, but she suddenly didn't want this man to think of her as some sort of freak.

"Seventeen," he repeated.

The hunger gave way to something else, she realized. The look on his face was curious . . . and calculating.

Suddenly, she realized what she'd just done.

She spun, snatching up the wet shirt and her shoes and stockings, tossing them all pell-mell into the basket.

"Wait!"

He grabbed her arm, and she jerked away, residual desire and fresh fear pumping adrenaline through her system. He was not holding her very tightly, and panic made her overzealous. Her foot slid on a wet rock, and she fell into the shallow stream.

The cold water was a shock, especially after the heat of the summer sun—and the scorch of her body's reaction to Stephen.

She struggled to get up, the quickly-soaking dress weighing heavily around her. Embarrassment warred with the need to get away.

Stephen reached down, putting both hands on her waist and lifting her up as if she weighed nothing. He put her on her bare feet, on the soft grass by the bank of the water. He didn't move his hands. She could feel the heat radiating from his palms through the damp material of her dress.

She held her breath.

Then, slowly, she reached out, putting her hands on his forearms. She imagined herself pushing out of his grip, slamming his hands away from her. Instead, her fingertips traced the muscles bunching beneath the cloth of his shirt. She touched him loosely, her palms resting on him.

He took a tentative step forward. She tilted her head back to get a better look into his face, so much higher than her own.

It must have looked like an invitation was her last conscious thought before his face leaned down and his mouth covered hers. She supposed, on some level, it was.

His lips were warm and firm against hers, and her whole body zinged with electricity. Her fingers dug into his wrists, capturing him rather than trying to evade. He molded her body to his, not caring that her soggy clothes pressed against him. She felt his rock-hard chest crush her breasts and the flesh between her thighs twitched in anticipation. She pressed harder against him, making low, throaty noises of need that she wasn't even aware of.

He must have known what her body so obviously craved. His mouth opened, forcing her lips to follow his, and his tongue darted forward, caressing the sensitive skin of her mouth. She gasped in surprise, a sound that quickly turned into a sigh of pleasure as his tongue started moving slowly, rhythmically in and out, taunting her tongue, beckoning her to follow his example. She pressed her legs tightly together, craving pressure against the pulsing sensation there. Her hands crept up to his shoulders, balancing herself against him. His hands moved forward to cup her buttocks, lifting her just enough to mold her body to his.

The thrill of his body pressed against hers caused a heated commotion to blast through every one of her nerve endings. She rubbed her pelvis against his, registering the hard length of his penis, straining against the front of his trousers. She wanted him, she realized as the kiss deepened, their tongues gradual in-and-out motion a precursor to the joining they were headed toward. Her pussy was wet, slick with need, her clit throbbing.

"Stephen," she breathed, tearing her mouth away from his. "*Stephen.*"

"I want you, too," he said, his voice a low growl. "God, I want you. Tell me where we can go."

She blinked, trying to make sense of his statement when all her body wanted him to do was take her, right there on the bank . . . strip off her clothes, strip off his own, and press his cock deep inside her, satisfying the ache that tortured her beyond sanity. She made a low whimpering sound, trying to reignite the kiss, trying to get them back on track.

"We can't stay here," he said, and there was both masculine amusement and raw desire in his voice. "Someone might see . . ."

It was the phrase that slapped her back into reality, and she took a stumbling step away from him, pressing a hand to her tight breasts, feeling her heart hammer beneath her palm.

Someone might see.

Someone might have already seen. Was she *trying* to get punished? Or, worse, banished? Was she willing to throw away ten years of anonymous sanctuary just to feel a man's cock inside her—no matter how he drew her, no matter how brutal her desire felt?

She felt tears prickling at the corners of her eyes.

"I have to go," she said. When he reached for her, she tugged herself away, as she should have from the beginning. "No! I can't be with you!"

She gathered up her things, and ran from the river, her body feverish and pained from unfulfilled passion. Her lips tingled, like the aftertaste of fire-hot chili, mixed with the rich sweetness of chocolate. She brushed the tears away with the back of her hand.

"Goodmaid Beth? What in God's name has happened?"

She glanced toward the new voice, startled. "Founder Amos?"

The Founder was staring at her legs. She realized that in her haste, she'd left her legs bared, her sleeves rolled up. A blatant disregard for the tenets. She turned from him, trying to get herself back into some semblance of decency.

"What is the meaning of this?"

"I was just washing clothes when, er, I slipped and fell in," she improvised, turning back to him. Her feet were still bare, but it would take too long to lace her shoes up. It couldn't be helped. She must look hideous, she thought.

"Fell in?" He sounded incredulous. And something else, something she couldn't put her finger on.

Her mind raced. "I guess I got clumsy," she said. It sounded stupid and utterly unbelievable. "I'm sorry. It won't happen again."

He frowned, his eyes going narrow behind his round wire-rimmed glasses. "Were you by yourself, Goodmaid Beth?"

Fear gripped her. "No, Founder Amos."

"Who else was with you?" This time, his usually cheerful voice sounded stern . . . menacing.

She started to speak, but choked. "The other Goodmaids," she said. "Washing clothes. They're still there."

He still looked suspicious, and she felt like guilt was painted across her face. But she couldn't bring herself to reveal her interaction with Stephen. Not only because of her own actions, but because the thought of anything happening to Stephen was more than she could bear.

Where can we go? he had asked.

Nowhere, she thought. There was nowhere safe.

"Go about your chores," Founder Amos instructed. "And from now on, don't break the rule: flesh is a beacon for impurity, and a Goodmaid is covered, from toe to wrist to neck, at all times."

She had noticed that he had not been able to tear his gaze away from her bare feet. She crossed them, nodding yet keeping her head down. "Yes, Founder," she mumbled.

She hurried away, barely registering that Founder Amos was heading toward the stream . . . and Stephen.

Stephen lingered by the small river, trying to be meditative about what had just happened, trying to get his raging hard-on to back off and give him a break.

What the hell is wrong with you?

He was here for a story, not to get laid. But from the minute she'd revealed she wanted him, all thoughts of work had disappeared, and all he could think about was getting this woman hot and naked underneath him, slipping himself into her slick folds and thrusting into her until they both lost themselves in passion.

Even more surprising was that she was still a virgin. She wasn't playing some well-practiced game with him, no fake little-girl coyness that he'd seen so many other women trot out like it was some kind of selling point. "Beth" might be inexperienced, but she was honest. Her desire for him was written in every trembling touch she laid on him. He felt overwhelmed by the fact that she'd obviously never broken the rules of the Compound before, and that something about him drew her, just as strongly as he was drawn.

He was too old, too seasoned a reporter, and too damned jaded to believe in bullshit like "love at first sight." But whatever this feeling he had for Beth was, it was a new one, and a powerful one. He didn't understand it, and frankly, it was starting to unnerve him.

"Goodman Stephen."

Stephen looked up, startled. "Huh?"

It was one of the Founders . . . Amos, he remembered slowly. The de facto leader of the seven Founders. The guy looked irritated.

No. The guy looked pissed. Stephen straightened.

"You should be working, Goodman Stephen," Amos scolded.

Stephen bit back a sigh. "I couldn't figure out which chore assignment I was in," Stephen lied glibly. "It's so peaceful here, I thought I might take a moment to sit by the stream and . . . reflect."

Which wasn't exactly lying, now that he thought about it.

"You are supposed to be helping to mend the fence, by the river's source," Founder Amos said. His eyes communicated clearly that he wasn't buying a word of Stephen's story. "However, I think from now on you'll be on off-Compound work detail."

Stephen frowned. "I'm sorry?"

"The mines," Founder Amos clarified. "We send several of our men to work out in the mines. Their income supplements the Compound."

Stephen knew that. He just hadn't realized that he might be set up for the work detail. Newcomers usually worked on the farm until they knew what was expected of them. "If that's what's best," Stephen said, keeping his voice neutral. It was obviously best that he stay away from Beth—during the day, anyway, when they could be seen.

Which just left the night. His body stiffened at the thought.

Amos's pale blue eyes went icy. "Watch yourself, Goodman Stephen."

Stephen wondered if the Founder had somehow read his mind.

"The women are washing the clothes today," Amos continued, and Stephen relaxed . . . until Amos's next statement. "Any man caught interfering with, harassing, or ogling the Goodmaids might find himself publicly punished, as a reminder that we've sworn to cast out the lustfulness and evil of the outside world."

Stephen realized the guy suspected or even knew about his little interaction with Beth. No, he couldn't know. Otherwise, his threat would be fact.

"I see," Stephen said, in that same toneless voice.

"You'd better." Although short in stature and generally harmless looking, Stephen suddenly realized that the Founder of the Penitents was less jovial than he'd initially read him as. There was steel beneath that Amish-teddy-bear exterior. The guy had a liberal dose of crazy mixed in with all that charm.

Founder Amos polished his glasses on the edge of his sleeve, then put them back on the bridge of his nose.

"It would be especially bad," he warned softly, "if anything involving Goodmaid Beth were to come to my attention."

Stephen's eyebrows jumped up.

"She is under the Founders' special care. She cleans our house, and we have watched her—that is, *protected* her— since she arrived, ten years ago, not much more than a child." Founder Amos was obviously trying to sound paternal, but there was a raw edge of something more possessive in his voice. "Her past is troubled, though she never speaks of it, and I am very, very protective of her. Do we have an understanding?"

"Yes," Stephen answered, his mind clicking. The guy wasn't just rabid about controlling the sexuality and conformity of his followers. The old bastard actually had a thing for Beth—and God help any young, new "stud" that might try and seduce Founder's beautiful little Goodmaid.

"Excellent." Amos pointed to the Commons. "I'll accompany you to your work team."

Stephen walked next to the Founder, thoughtful.

Ten years. She'd been seventeen, ten years ago.

Seventeen years old, with eyes like crushed wet violets . . .

He actually stopped in his tracks.

Founder Amos frowned at him. "Something amiss?" he asked, his voice rolling with sarcasm.

"Huh? Uh, no. Sorry." Stephen kept walking, even as his mind raced.

No way. Couldn't be her. She's an urban myth. A legend.

If she was who his memory was suggesting . . . well, hell. She'd be the biggest story of his career.

But there was no way that beautiful, earnest little virgin was a princess. He shook his head, following the Founder. His mind was playing tricks on him. The sooner he could get out of this place—and away from her—the better off he'd be.

Chapter Four

"Goodmaid Beth? Are you all right?"

Beth looked up from the pot she was scrubbing. "I'm sorry. What?"

Goodmaid Amelia, an older woman with a broad, chubby face was staring at her with concern. "I asked, are you feeling well? You look dazed."

Beth shook her head. "I had trouble sleeping," she admitted.

She'd barely slept at all. Obsessively, her mind had played and replayed her hot, torturous kiss with Stephen by the riverbank. The way his hands had held her, the way his mouth had melded to hers. It was enough to make her pause in whatever she was doing, shivering as the memory washed over her like rain. Her body throbbed, one large, unfulfilled ache.

He'd wanted to get her alone. And she wanted nothing more than to be alone with him.

Beth lingered over the cleanup, not wanting to go outside where she might run into him. She didn't know what she'd do. There was just something about him, something that she couldn't resist. Her body cried out for his, but more than that . . . he was easy to talk to. And for the first time in a long time, she felt like finally revealing some of the secrets she'd been hiding for so many years.

Stephen had just joined the Penitents, and no one, to her knowledge, ever left. They might be banished—a real threat for herself, she realized, if she continued on this dangerous, lust-ridden path—but no one left of his own accord, not in the ten years since she'd first walked through the high gate and entered the Compound. Which meant she might be tortured by his presence for years, as the pressure mounted with each passing day.

Something had to be done. She just had no idea what.

"I'll take care of the rest of the kitchen cleanup, Goodmaid Beth," a woman's voice said pleasantly. "We're expecting a food delivery anyway, and it's my job to go over the list."

Beth turned, then realized who had spoken to her. It was Lydia—the one she'd seen with Goodman Henry, out in the meadow. Beth barely recognized her. Lydia's veil was on, her face was placid as a plaster saint's. Her dress was buttoned as high as it could possibly go. She was the picture of humility, the embodiment of all that was Penitent.

Beth cleared her throat. "I'll just finish up cleaning the counters," she said slowly.

Lydia frowned slightly. "All right. But you know the

Founders don't want Goodmaids interacting with people from outside the Compound, if it can be helped. Even if the delivery person is a woman." With that warning, Lydia disappeared out of the kitchen, waiting at the delivery entrance by the pantry.

Beth stared at Lydia's retreating form. Just looking at her, no one would suspect that Lydia was living a lurid double life. She seemed above reproach. She was apparently a brilliant actress. And Lydia had been a member of the Penitents for over a year. How long had she been "enjoying" herself on the sly?

And how had she managed to keep it so quiet?

Beth finished wiping down the counters, then found herself following the red-haired woman. She wasn't sure how to approach her, or when she did, what question she might ask.

How do you have sex here, in the Penitent Compound, of all places?

Beth felt the slow burn of a blush heat her cheeks, and she ducked into the pantry, hiding behind a large bank of shelves stocked with dry beans and canned goods. Even if she asked Lydia the question, what would she do with the answer?

A truck rumbled up to the delivery entrance, brakes screeching to a halt. "You're new," she heard Lydia say, her voice sharp. "What happened to Elise?"

Beth stood still, realizing that Lydia must be talking to the outsider, the delivery woman. The delivery woman laughed, sounding more like a cackle. "Elise found a better job. Don't worry, though, girlie, she let me in on the scam before she left."

Scam? Beth listened intently. The delivery woman's voice

was rough, as if rasped raw from years of smoking and drinking. She sounded older, gravelly and a little husky. Beth frowned, straining to listen.

"Not so loud," Lydia hissed. "Do you have the stuff?" She sounded excited.

Beth wondered if Lydia were buying drugs. Was there any vice the woman didn't indulge in?

"Right here." There was a crinkling sound, and Beth tried to crane her head around a jar of kidney beans to see what was going on. She didn't see what had changed hands, but she did see who Lydia was talking to.

The delivery woman was easily in her fifties or sixties. She had a thin, willowy body, despite the bulky work clothes and heavy boots she was wearing. Her hair flopped in front of her face, dyed an ashy blond at some point but revealing three inches of tangled gray roots. All these were minor details.

Her face . . .

One of the woman's cheekbones sat precariously lower than the other, almost sunken in, and the heavy wrinkled folds around her eyes made them seem even more deep set than nature had originally made them. Loose jowls hung around her chin, despite her thinness. Her lips were malformed, her lower lip large but not full, as if some drunken artist had painted a dark pink smear over her chin. And her nose angled awkwardly, as if it were half sliding from her face.

Beth couldn't help staring, letting out a tiny, surprised gasp.

Lydia stiffened, then turned toward Beth's hiding place. Beth ducked back quickly. There was a sound of footsteps;

then Lydia was in front of her, eyes blazing with anger—and fear. "What are you doing here?"

Beth cleared her throat. "I was . . . I was just . . ." Her mind couldn't come up with a suitable lie.

Lydia stood close to Beth, towering several inches taller than her. "This doesn't concern you," Lydia said, and her voice was haughty. "As I said, the Founders would not want you interacting with an outsider. They've entrusted this job to me . . . and I'm sure they would be very, very unhappy if they found out you've disobeyed them."

Beth's eyes narrowed. She wouldn't have expected threats from Lydia, not before the meadow incident. Now, she realized the Goodmaid with the quiet demeanor and serene appearance obviously had a lot of hidden capabilities.

"Do you understand?" Lydia stepped a little closer, until she was right in Beth's face.

"I understand that if I say anything about what I've just seen, you'll be punished. Maybe even banished," Beth said instead. She might be afraid of some things—banishment and death at her stepmother's hand topping the list—but she was hardly intimidated by a young woman who acted like a saint in public but was obviously used to lying and cheating to get her way. Beth decided to throw in a threat of her own. "Not to mention your fondness for the meadow."

Lydia went pale. "I don't know what you're talking about," she said, her voice cracking.

"I'm sure you do," Beth replied. "Don't worry, I'm not going to turn you in. But don't threaten me." She paused. "Since we're on the subject, I need to ask you something."

Lydia's eyes widened in surprise, but she recovered with remarkable speed. "All right," she said, her voice business-like and brisk. "What do you want?"

"What's all this?" The delivery woman walked to where Beth and Lydia were standing. Then she stared openly at Beth, her malformed mouth falling slightly agape.

Beth winced. She was used to scrutiny—her face was un-usual enough to generate stares. She shifted her gaze to the floor, hoping, as always, that she wouldn't be recognized. Since she'd staged her death, she hoped that the tabloids had finally lost their interest, and since she'd aged, she hoped no one would be able to connect her seventeen-year-old face to what she looked like now. A few people might think she looked familiar, but none of them would actually believe she was the same person.

"Don't worry," Lydia said. "She's not going to say any-thing. She was just about to tell me what she wanted in ex-change for keeping quiet."

That wasn't actually what Beth was going to do, but she felt too flustered to argue. She didn't bother to look at the delivery woman. "We'll talk later," she said instead, feeling uncomfortable. She didn't mean to blackmail anyone . . . she just wanted some answers, to questions she wasn't even sure she'd be able to ask.

The delivery woman put a hand on Beth's wrist, stop-ping her. The hand was clawlike, lined with veins, darkened with liver spots. "Is there anything I can tempt you with, dearie?"

Beth turned, startled. "What?"

"Some chocolate, maybe?" The woman's watery gray eyes

were intent. "Booze? Cigarettes? Some lingerie?" She cackled. "You strike me as the type who might like to wear something a little more racy under all that gray."

Beth's eyes widened, and she looked at Lydia, stunned.

"Lydia, here, has a system," the woman said, her face twisting into a smug expression. "She over orders, and the Founders pay . . . but we don't deliver everything. I pocket the difference. In exchange, Lydia gets some trinkets that she wants."

Lydia's face flushed pink with silent anger.

"So, if you keep your pretty mouth shut," the woman continued, "I'm sure Lydia wouldn't mind if you got a few little treats of your own. Here." She reached into her pocket, then grabbed Beth's hand again, pressing a few small items into her palm. "First time's free." She cackled again, sounding like a hag from a children's story, then she left the pantry.

Beth opened her hand, reluctantly curious. The woman had given her a small gold-paper-wrapped chocolate truffle. Alongside the truffle were two foil-wrapped condoms.

Beth dropped them as if they were snakes.

"Damn her," Lydia hissed. Then she looked at Beth. "You didn't need to know all of that. You aren't going to go running out, blabbing to the Founders, are you?"

"Uh . . ." Beth's head was swimming.

"Just tell me what you want. I'll get it for you."

Beth looked down at the contraband she'd dropped. Slowly, she picked up the chocolate. It was forbidden on the Compound. It was too decadent, too reminiscent of lust and physical pleasure. But oh, how she'd remembered loving the taste of it as a child!

Lydia smiled. "I'll get you all the truffles you want."

Beth blushed. "I won't turn you in," she said, and realized she meant it. It wasn't her business. "But you should be careful."

Then she stared at the condoms, watching as Lydia scooped them up. Lydia must have seen something in her expression, because she held out her hand.

"You sure you don't want one?"

Her voice was mocking, and Beth turned, rushing away. It had taken all she had, not to grab one of the foil packets.

She sneaked back to her room, unwrapping the truffle, taking one careful nibble out of the edge. When the rich taste rolled over her tongue, she wriggled with pleasure.

Maybe I should've taken the condom.

She closed her eyes. She'd already taken one small step down the road of temptation. It was going to be a slippery slope from there.

"How long have you been with the Penitents?" Stephen asked his dinner companions.

"Three years," Goodman Joshua, to his left, said. The guy was built like a beefy linebacker, but had a strange gentleness that suited the agricultural society well. He was soft-spoken and somewhat shy.

"I've been here since they started the place, fifteen years ago now," the old geezer across from him said proudly. His name was Goodman Eamon. Stephen got the feeling it wasn't the name he was born with. He was a walking encyclopedia of Penitent lore.

Between the two of them, Stephen felt confident that he had the story behind the camp. He'd already written the lead in his mind. With any luck, he'd be out of here within a day. Two, tops.

His gaze stole over to the women's side of the building. Beth was sitting next to a plump-faced older woman, who was laughing softly at something another woman was saying. Beth simply smiled, a small, beautiful smile, tinged with melancholy.

That look tugged at his memory, yet again. *It's not the legendary princess. Will you knock it off?*

Of course, he wasn't just looking at her because she reminded him of a tabloid paper's dream.

"You'd better stop doing that," Eamon warned him.

Stephen's eyes snapped forward. "What? What'd I do?"

"She causes all sorts of trouble for men when they first get here," Brother Joshua said, with sympathy. "Being so pretty, and all."

"Temptation." Eamon clucked his tongue reprovingly. "Never shoulda let her in . . . but she was a lot younger then. A little less . . ." He made a motion with his hands.

"Enticing?" Stephen supplied, then winced. He hadn't meant to offer that word up, but it did cover what he felt about her. Enticing. Compelling. Entrancing. *Take your pick.*

He had to get out of here.

"She's a good girl, though," Joshua piped in. "She never, you know, tries to . . . er, *entice* anybody."

"Doesn't matter," Eamon countered. "Her very presence here is a temptation. I know, Founder Amos thinks that having her among us makes us stronger . . . by fighting the attraction daily."

Stephen nodded, taking a bite of roast beef. He knew he sure felt that way . . . struggling against the temptation she presented, on a minute-by-minute basis.

"It's not her fault," Joshua continued, stubbornly. It was maybe the most that Stephen had ever heard the giant man speak. Apparently, he had a jones for Goodmaid Beth as well. "I mean, she was born that way. And she came here, right?"

There was that. What *had* brought her here? Stephen wondered for the millionth time.

Eamon sighed heavily. "I just think we'd all be better off if she would just be banished, and be done with it."

"Banishment," Stephen said slowly. "What does that entail, exactly?"

That shut the two other men up momentarily. Joshua looked a little nervous. Even Eamon shifted his weight on his wooden bench.

"I've only seen two people banished in the time I've been here," Eamon said uncomfortably. "And that was twelve years ago. It's not done lightly."

Stephen nodded. He'd heard of banishment, or "shunning," in other cults he'd researched. It involved cutting someone off from the community, forbidding any contact with them. Considering, Stephen could hardly see how that'd be such a bad thing. He might work on getting banished, himself, as an easy way to get out of this joint and on to his next assignment.

"I've only heard about it," Joshua said, and Stephen could've sworn the big man shuddered.

"What's the big deal?" Stephen asked, puzzled at their extreme reactions.

The two men looked around, making sure nobody heard his rash comment. "You don't ever want to be banished," Eamon said darkly. "Believe me. It's not what you'd think . . . and it's reserved for only the very worst of transgressions."

"Better beaten than banished," Joshua agreed, and it sounded like he was quoting something.

"They beat people here?" Stephen's eyes widened.

"Sure." Eamon scooped up a forkful of mashed potatoes, obviously more comfortable with the subject of beatings. And if that wasn't weird, Stephen didn't know what was. "Again, just when people deserve it. You know—talking to the opposite gender, shirking your work, making contact with outsiders. Stuff like that."

Stephen nodded again, just to keep the old guy going. This was shaping up to be a better story than he'd thought, but a lot of it was unsubstantiated.

His eyes crept over to Beth again. She looked away quickly, and his heart pounded quicker.

"Has Beth ever been punished?" he asked quietly.

Eamon snorted. "Hardly. She's one of the Founders' favorites. They coddle her."

"She's a good girl," Joshua said.

"I'll bet they probably don't punish women as much, anyway," Stephen said, shrugging, trying to fight the urge to stare at her.

"Actually, Goodmaids are punished far more," Eamon said. "Since they're much more susceptible to temptation."

Stephen fought the urge to roll his eyes. He ate the rest

of his dinner, listening to his two dining companions talk about the nature of temptation and vice, resisting the siren call of Beth's presence as best he could.

When he left here, he wanted to think he could shake her off, the way he'd moved on from women—and stories— before. He wanted to believe that he could just bury himself in the next assignment, and her violet eyes would just be a fleeting memory, something he thought of at random when he saw a movie or maybe the purplish blue of the night sky. But some part of him knew he was just trying to fool himself. She was already beginning to haunt him, and he was afraid that, once he left, she'd become an obsession . . . one that no other woman could ever live up to.

He got up, his tray clacking on the table.

"Finished already?" Eamon said, surprised.

"You can't leave," Joshua protested, as Stephen headed for the door. "Founder Amos is going to lecture tonight . . ."

But Stephen needed air. He walked out into the twilight, watching as the sunset bled a deep orange-crimson behind the trees.

For the first time in a long time, he wasn't sure what to do. He knew what he ought to do: dig up whatever dirt he needed to, finish the story, and get the hell out. But what his mind knew, and what his body was trying to convince him to do, were two completely different things.

He didn't know how long he walked, but he turned when he heard a small voice behind him, in the growing darkness.

"Over here."

He squinted, peering in the shadows behind the Dining Hall.

It was Beth.

His heart started to beat faster, and he walked over to her quickly. "Why, Goodmaid Beth, you shouldn't . . ."

"Do you want me?"

He blinked at her, startled. "Are you kidding?"

She looked pained.

"Of course I want you," he heard himself say.

"Then we have to talk," she said, her voice barely audible. "Meet me, at midnight. There's a meadow, just north of here." She pointed. "About twenty minutes into the woods. I'll be waiting."

With that, she disappeared back into the Dining Hall kitchen, where the flurry of sound suggested that she was helping clean up.

He stood for a moment, beyond stunned.

This wasn't helping his case any, his mind pointed out dryly. But his body was already too far gone to listen to it. He knew exactly where he'd be at midnight.

Beth waited for Stephen in the pale moonlight. Ever since she'd witnessed the tryst between Lydia and Henry, the meadow no longer felt like hers, and no longer held the tranquility she once associated with it.

After tonight, she thought, that tranquility might never return. She would always associate the place with Stephen . . . and the decision she had to make.

Of course I want you.

She closed her eyes. His words made her shiver, her stomach clenching tightly . . . her pussy going damp. This was why they had to meet. They had to talk. They couldn't go on for years with this powerful, undeniable attraction going on between them.

She didn't know what they could do about it, but she wasn't leaving that meadow until she—they—figured something out.

"I was wondering if you'd really be here."

Stephen's voice caught her off guard, and she turned, her heart hammering in her chest. He stepped out of the shadows. He was dressed in his day clothes, the buttons of his shirt opened a little and the sleeves rolled up, a nod to the summer heat. His blond hair was rumpled, looking utterly touchable. She had the impulsive desire to run her fingers through the wavy mass.

She cleared her throat. "We have to talk," she said.

"Really." His voice was a purr. "You wanted me to meet you here . . . to talk?"

She took a step back, his words rubbing over her like mink over naked skin. She trembled. "We can't just keep going on like this."

"Like what? I've only seen you twice." His smile seeped warmth right into her bones. "And I've only kissed you once . . ."

He took a step closer to her, and she stepped out of the edge of the meadow, using the trees as a sort of hiding place, trying to keep him from getting too close.

"That's the problem," she said. "We want each other. I can't believe how much I'm feeling, and that's after only two occasions. We're going to be spending our whole *lives* here, Goodman Stephen. This can't continue!"

He looked surprised, and then his face turned impassive. "What's your solution?"

She took a deep breath. "We could try avoiding each other. Deliberately. Make sure we never see each other."

He was following her, just a few steps behind. Part of her wanted to stand still, let him catch her. And then what?

"Do you really think that would work?" he asked.

She closed her eyes. "No," she said honestly. Even when she hadn't seen him, she'd thought about him to distraction.

"What's your next option?"

She swallowed nervously. "I don't know. I was hoping you could help me come up with something," she pleaded. "You joined the Penitents for a reason. Do you really want to spend years dodging this?" She paused, and then plowed forward: "Or giving in to . . . to our physical attraction, and then facing each other day after day? To maybe get caught, punished, possibly even banished? I mean . . . is it really worth it?"

She hoped she was appealing to his sense of reason. But his eyes gleamed in the dim light, and his smile was mesmerizing.

"You would be worth it," he breathed.

No one had ever looked at her that way before. No one had ever made her feel that way . . . so desirable. So worthwhile.

They stood like that, silent, with waves of sexual tension stretching the short distance between their bodies like live wires. She didn't know how long they remained in stasis, but slowly, she heard sounds invading the meadow.

"Someone's coming," she whispered, fear flooding her system. They both chose the same tree to hide behind, diving for the same spot. He wound up crushing her against the bark of the same gnarled oak she'd hidden behind, that fateful night. Visions of the Founders or Goodmen on patrol sprang to mind. She tried to stay as small and unnoticeable as possible, clinging to Stephen unconsciously, breathing in his masculine scent as it mixed with the scents of the surrounding pine and the thick, humid air.

Tentatively, Stephen put a palm on her waist. She took a quick, silent gasp, but otherwise made no sign of protest.

The flesh between her legs started to throb.

"Hurry." A woman's voice. Women were not allowed on patrol—it was a man's duty, per the Founders. So whoever it was, wasn't supposed to be out, either.

Beth felt relief, like a tidal wave crashing through her. She didn't move her hand from Stephen's chest, though.

"We don't have all night, Henry."

It was Lydia again, Beth realized, swallowing a nervous laugh. They were having another meadow tryst. It would be funny, except . . .

She held her breath. Except now, she was going to listen to them having sex again, go through all those sensations—*with Stephen right in front of her,* his body only inches away from hers. . . .

She closed her eyes, gritting her teeth. She could put up with a lot. She *had* endured a lot of deprivation in the ten years since she'd joined the Penitents. But this might be more temptation than she could refuse.

Stephen was initially puzzled by what he was hearing. What, exactly, was going on here?

"I got here as quickly as I could, Lydia," the man referred to as Henry said, his voice tense. "But it's getting more dangerous. There's rumor that the fence patrols are going to start searching the grounds . . ."

"Patrols. What a joke," Lydia scoffed. "Two heavyset, middle-aged men taking the occasional stroll."

"They caught Goodmaid Jessica a few years ago," Henry pointed out.

Stephen felt Beth stiffen against him, and he stroked her waist, trying to comfort her. She went still beneath his fingertips, but he could still feel the heat radiating from her skin, practically scorching him.

"She was trying to tackle the barbed-wire fence," Lydia said. "Besides, she's a clumsy cow, and a pathetic one besides. If she was really so unhappy, there were other options she could have taken. Now, are we going to talk all night, or are we going to do this?"

Henry laughed reluctantly. "Even when I was on the outside," he said, "I never met a woman as hungry for sex as you, Lydia."

Stephen's jaw fell open. Here? A nympho, in Celibacy Central?

He bit back on a laugh, his body convulsing as he forced himself to stay silent. He barely caught a look at Beth's surprised, alarmed expression when he shook his head, then buried his face in the crook of her neck to muffle any further sounds. She was still wearing her veil, so his forehead was pressed against the flesh of her collarbone, and the brief expanse of skin just below her jaw. He took a shallow breath and inhaled her flower-scented essence.

Abruptly, all humor fled, replaced by an even more compelling emotion.

Beth shifted, her breasts brushing against the planes of his chest. That slight motion caused the hardening of his body to accelerate.

"Maybe we should keep some clothes on tonight, Lydia . . ."

"Coward." The word was taunting. It was followed by the sound of rustling. "You know I like to feel your skin sliding against mine. Besides—you're going to be in for a treat tonight."

"Really?" Henry sounded intrigued.

"It's a surprise."

Stephen sneaked a look around the tree trunk. The woman had shucked out of her clothes and veil and was standing naked in the middle of the clearing, her breasts full and jutting out, nipples erect. She was stretching out on the pile of discarded clothing, her hands beckoning to the man. The man was quickly following suit, stripping off his shirt and pants, his cock sticking out like a weather vane. He stepped toward Lydia, and she curled her hand around his hard-on with a confident stroke.

"We have to be careful, Lydia," the man sent one more reminder before tilting his head back and closing his eyes, getting on his knees. "Oh, that feels so damned *good* . . ."

"Hurry," Lydia repeated, spreading her thighs and letting him lie between them. "I don't want to share you just yet."

"Share me . . . ?"

Stephen heard Beth gasp, and he looked away from the sexual scene playing out in front of him. Her mouth was moving—she was whispering something, but he couldn't hear what. He leaned down, his body still pressed hard against hers. Her lips brushed against his ear.

"Are there only two of them there?" she whispered.

"Wait!" Henry said, his voice breathless. "Did you hear that?"

Stephen and Beth both held their breath, pressing against the tree trunk, trying to disappear against it. Stephen could feel the beat of Beth's heart. She crushed her breasts against him, her hips fitted to his as he covered her against the tree.

"There's no one out there," Lydia responded, sounding irritated, "and you're ruining my mood."

"Well, we don't want that."

There was silence for a second . . . then moist noises, mingled with groans from Henry, and little excited panting noises from Lydia. Stephen wondered if they should try to take advantage of their distraction, and leave. He carefully brushed his own lips against Beth's ear. "Should we—"

"Ow!" Lydia yelled. "Damn it, pay attention!"

"I thought I heard something!"

Stephen sighed. They couldn't risk it. He could tell from Beth's tension that she realized it, too. They would simply have to wait it out.

The sounds of sexual activity started up again. "Like that," Lydia instructed him, her voice imperious. "Harder. I want to feel your cock pounding inside of me." Henry groaned in response, and from Lydia's deep, rippling moan, Stephen had to guess she'd gotten what she wanted.

Stephen abruptly realized that he was still pressed against Beth—and that his own cock was hard with need. Just thinking about Beth always had him semi-erect, but being this close to her, breathing in her perfume, feeling the heated softness of her body just inches away from his, was almost more than his body could take. His hard-on started to throb.

Beth was breathing shallowly, and he could feel her nipples, like pebbles, poking through the thick cotton of her nightgown.

He didn't want to scare her. Considering she'd spoken of how they'd deny what they felt, he knew that she didn't necessarily want a physical relationship—but then she'd admitted to how strongly her body reacted to his. From the feel of her, and the way she clung to him, he wondered if her body was as aroused as his was. How much sway did her body have over her logic?

His hand traced up from her waist, only the barest of inches, along her rib cage. She was so slight, so delicate. He could feel the shift of fabric against skin, burning his fingertips with her heat. It was only the tiniest of caresses, and he stared at her face, giving her plenty of room to stop him.

She froze instead, and he paused, unsure of whether or not he should continue. Then, almost imperceptibly, she angled her body. His fingertips brushed the soft swell on the underside of her breast. For someone so small, her breasts were full and high, tantalizing him. He stroked the underside experimentally, still slow, still hesitant. She was still frozen, and he thought he could see her throat work convulsively. Nonetheless, she didn't move away.

He wondered at her experience. The other men had suggested that no one had given in to her wiles. He realized that, because of her striking beauty, they couldn't imagine that she *didn't* have wiles. Especially not in a place like this . . .

although, given what was happening out in the meadow, he couldn't discount the possibility.

He cupped Beth's breast more fully, tracing the areola with his thumb, flicking the hardness of the erect nipple. Beth let out the tiniest of sounds, a quick, sharp mewl of pleasure. She shifted, her breast pushing closer to his touch. Inadvertently, her hips slid against the hardness of his erection. He stifled a groan, putting his head down against her shoulder.

"Oh, God, yeah," Lydia gasped out in the meadow. "Fuck me, Henry. *Harder.*"

Stephen ignored what was going on, focusing his entire world on the woman pressed against him in the darkness. She turned her head. He could smell the sweetness of her breath, less than an inch from his own mouth. He leaned down, bridging the gap, feeling the softness of her lips against his own. She gasped into his mouth now, and he traced the outline of her sensuous pout with his tongue. She tasted delicious, like sweet cherry wine. He stroked the delicate inner flesh of her lips, then delved further. After a moment, her tongue crept out, hesitant, shy. He teased it with his own, and soon the two of them were kissing deeply, their bodies pressing together more tightly as his tongue dipped in, out, in a slow rhythm that reminded him of the joining he felt sure they both wanted.

"I want you to come, baby," Henry muttered, out in the meadow. The sound of their lovemaking had turned frantic, skin slapping against skin.

"I'm close," Lydia rasped. "Right there, oh, *oh* . . ."

Stephen felt like his blood was on fire. His hands roamed across Beth's frame, cupping her breasts, kneading them gently. Her fingers dug into his shoulders, lifting her, and she pushed herself further into his palms. She kissed him harder, devouring him with her sweet mouth, clinging to him as if she couldn't bear to be torn away.

His cock was hard as concrete, and his hands slid down her sides to grip her hips, angling her toward him, rubbing his erection against the juncture of her thighs. When she froze again, he realized that he'd gone too far, too quickly.

"I'm sorry," he breathed, his voice hoarse and low. The voices in the meadow were starting to get a little louder, a little throatier. Lydia was obviously close to hitting her orgasm.

"It's all right," Beth murmured back. "It's just . . . I've never . . ."

It took him a second to realize what she was telling him. *She was a virgin.*

He knew there were virgins, even in this day and age, but frankly, they struck him as a bit mythical. "Not in any way?" he whispered back furtively.

"Just kisses," Beth explained, her body grinding against his. "And that . . . was a long time ago . . ."

"Yes!" Lydia let out a subdued cry in the meadow. *"Yes! Yes! Yes!"*

Stephen shuddered, biting his lip. It shouldn't have made a difference, but knowing that all of this was new to her only increased his own frenzied desire for her. It also put it in perspective: she wanted him, and she'd had opportunities to be with any number of men. But she'd chosen *him.*

He felt humbled by the admission, and unsure of how to proceed.

"My turn," Henry in the meadow said smugly.

"Not quite yet," Lydia interrupted. "There's someone else here."

Stephen froze. Had they been caught?

Another woman's voice chimed in. "I can't believe you started without me," she said, her voice petulant.

"There's plenty to go around," Lydia said, laughing. "Come on, Camille. This is the man I was telling you about."

A threesome, Stephen thought quickly, in amused disbelief.

Then Beth shifted beneath him, and all thoughts of anyone else fled.

Beth could barely contain herself. The feel of Stephen against her was making her body explode with sensation. His kisses were drugging, intoxicating. She wanted to strip out of her rough cotton nightgown and feel his skin gliding against hers, feel the muscles of his body bunch and contract as he . . .

As he what? She knew what had to happen, but she'd never experienced, so she felt at a loss. What would it feel like, to have his cock parting her flesh, to feel her pussy filled with the hard length she'd felt pressed at the juncture of her thighs? She was breathless at the mere thought of it.

There were three voices in the meadow now. Backed against the tree, her gazed flitted over to them in distraction. She could see why none of the three participants would notice Stephen and her, hidden in the shadows. The group was far too intent on their own sexual pursuits. Lydia was naked— *as usual*, Beth thought with envy—her red hair looking black in what little light emerged from the pale silver of the waning moon. Henry was naked, as well, looking tall and lanky, ropy with muscle from working in the fields on the Compound. He was on his feet, his cock jutting out prominently as he stood there in the humid night.

"I told you I was going to bring someone else to play," Lydia said, her voice smug.

"I hope you don't mind," the third participant added.

Beth recognized the woman: Goodmaid Camille, who had been on the Compound for five years. She wasn't very pretty, but she was "built," her body full and curvaceous. She wore a broad, hungry smile. Henry didn't say anything in response—his face looked confused yet aroused by the goings-on.

Beth turned her focus back to Stephen, wondering if he were as surprised by the multiple participants as she. But when her gaze met his, she realized he was focused only on her. Her pulse pounded wildly in her throat. He leaned down, kissing the smile from her mouth.

"We might get caught . . ." she heard Henry say from the meadow, his tone nervous. Beth stiffened slightly, realizing they might *all* get caught, and turned to see what was going on. Stephen turned his attention to her neck, pressing soft, hot kisses from the sensitive spot behind her earlobe to the hollow of her collarbone, and she gasped silently.

Lydia made an impatient sound. She knelt in front of Henry, taking him into her mouth. He groaned softly, tilting his head back, pushing his hips toward her as his fingers twined in her hair, holding her head steady. Beth could hear the minute suckling sounds that Lydia made as she slowly worked on his erection.

Then Camille moved forward. She took off her clothes and veil, revealing pale blond hair that shone in the moonlight, a contrast to Lydia's darkness. She spooned behind Lydia, caressing Lydia's breast with one hand while the other hand burrowed between Lydia's thighs. Lydia's moan, muffled by Henry's cock, was one of intense pleasure. Camille was making little soft panting noises as well, kissing Lydia's back as her hips wiggled in obvious sensual torment.

Beth felt as if a trigger was released inside her. She wasn't interested in Lydia's sex games, but their complete abandon— their willingness to risk punishment in the name of pleasure— was riveting. Her body, already primed by Stephen's devoted kisses, started to flow wetly, her breasts heavy and throbbing, her stomach jittering with sexual energy. She stared at Stephen. He was ignoring the sex play. He only had eyes for her. He stared at her face, stroking her cheek softly.

She couldn't hold back any more. She kissed him hard, passion bursting inside her like a spring. He responded in kind. His fingers slid from her waist to cup her buttocks, lifting her slightly as she helped out eagerly, parting her thighs to gently straddle his trousered waist. His clothed cock rubbed hard against the nightgown that shielded her pussy, and she gasped silently, her nipples tingling, her whole body electrified. Impatiently he tugged up the hem of her gown . . . then his hand froze. She saw him staring at her, his face apologetic.

She paused for all of a second before she reached down, helping pull the gown the rest of the way, exposing her panties and bare legs. Then she buried her face against his shoulder.

His fingers explored her in the darkness, finding the top of her panties and reaching inside, stroking softly. She bit her lips as his fingers grazed through the thick curls covering her sex.

"Taste him," Beth heard Lydia saying, issuing orders like a director in a sexual stage play. Camille let out a cry of pleased surprise that turned into a muffled moan. Soon, the only sounds coming from the meadow were low groans of pleasure, the moist sounds of sex and the low cries of ecstasy.

Beth raised one leg, angling it to hook over Stephen's hip, parting herself even wider, making his access to her easier. She clung to his shoulders and let out a tiny cry as he traced her damp slot, parting the folds of skin. He dipped a finger inside her, tracing her, then delved deeper with slow thoroughness. She felt his touch like a hot brand, lancing her with sexual fire. She bit his shoulder through the cotton of his shirt, unable to stop herself from moving her hips to swivel against his searching fingers.

"That's it," Lydia said, out in the meadow. "Harder, baby. I want to feel you come inside me. . . ."

Beth gasped softly, pressing herself harder, biting her lip as Stephen's fingers penetrated deeper inside her. She leaned up closer to his face. "I want to feel you inside me," she echoed, barely audible.

He groaned softly against her, his body pressing against her as his fingers stroked inside her pussy. She shuddered at the sensation. Blindly, she kissed him, feeling his tongue sweep inside her mouth. Her tongue twined with his as his fingers withdrew and penetrated. She could feel the pressure building inside her, and she wrapped her leg around him, pulling him close.

Stephen's fingers started to move more quickly, and Beth's hips bucked against his fingers as she found herself twisting and writhing against him, her breathing quick and ragged. He withdrew his fingers, finding the little button of flesh at her opening. For a moment, she wished that he'd kneel down and taste her, replacing his fingers with teeth and tongue. Then, replacing his tongue with something even more substantial . . .

I want to feel you come inside me.

Instead, he gently but firmly rubbed her clit as his fingers pressed deeper inside her.

"Oh!"

She let the tiny sound out, unable to help herself. Fortunately, the threesome in the clearing didn't notice as they were close to finding their own release.

"*God,*" she heard Henry grunt roughly, as Lydia chanted, "Yes, ohhhh, *yes,*" and Camille simply made mewling sounds of kittenlike pleasure.

Stephen's fingers plunged into Beth, and she felt an explosion of sensation radiate through her. Her thighs crushed against his palm, and she felt a wave of wetness pour down as she shuddered against him, her body trembling uncontrollably. The orgasm rocked through her, and she made the tiniest cry as her muscles contracted against Stephen's searching hand.

She wished he were inside her.

"Lydia!"

Beth glanced over, dazed. Henry was behind Lydia, his cock penetrating her as she knelt, her head obscured by Camille's parted thighs. The man was pumping his way to fulfillment and Lydia still managed to rear back against him. He shuddered, slamming against her, and she clawed at his thighs, lifting her head long enough to cry out *"YES!"* They shuddered together. Camille made a small sound of protest until Lydia knelt back down, with Henry still inside her, and burrowed her head back between Camille's thighs. Within moments, Camille's breathing went heavy and labored, and she let out a rippling cry, her thighs circling Lydia's red hair.

The meadow finally went silent except for the sounds of rasping breaths. Lydia was the first to speak. "Fucking marvelous," she commented, causing Henry and Camille to laugh.

Stephen leaned down, kissing Beth gently before withdrawing his hand from between her thighs. She could still feel the hardness of his cock against her stomach, and she traced it through the fabric of his pants with the tips of her fingers. He shivered, moving her hand away. She bit her lip, embarrassed. He simply pressed her hand to his lips, kissing her fingertips gently. "Wait," he breathed against her ear.

After long minutes, the group in the clearing got their clothes back on. "See? We didn't get caught," Lydia said triumphantly to Henry.

"When can we meet again?" Camille asked, almost desperately.

"Maybe tomorrow," Lydia said.

"You're playing it too close to the edge," Henry warned.

Lydia laughed. "That's okay. Camille and I can play without you." The voices trailed off as the three of them made their way back to the dorms.

"I can't believe that just happened," Beth said finally, when the coast was clear.

"Which part?" Stephen asked, his voice gently teasing.

Beth could feel a blush heat her cheeks. "Them," she clarified, then shook her head. "And . . . us."

He kissed her. "I didn't mean to stop you," he said. "But . . . I know you're not that experienced. And I don't want your first time to be quick."

She smiled at him, and he stared at her mouth hungrily.

"But I do want your first time to be with me."

"So do I," she breathed.

He sighed. "Which means we've got to get you out of here."

She blinked, surprised at his abrupt change of topic.

"It's not an easy place to get out of," he noted. "But we can do it. I can help you. I can help you on the outside, too. You can stay with me, until we figure out what you're going to do next."

"Why are you helping me?" she asked. In her experience, no one was altruistic. She'd had to pay every cent she had to escape from her stepmother's clutches, leaving her penniless and vulnerable—which was how she'd wound up here, at the Penitent Compound. She wanted to trust Stephen, but didn't know how.

His eyes were thoughtful.

"I don't know," he answered, and his voice sounded tortured. "Now . . . go on. Go to bed, before I lose whatever weird nobility I seem to have developed."

She did as he asked, walking away on shaky legs.

"Beth?" he called out, stopping her.

She turned back, nodding.

"Maybe we should find someplace else to meet," he said, and she grinned ruefully.

"My room is the farthest west, in the women's dorm," she said. "We can meet in the woods by there, if you like."

"All right," he agreed. "Then . . . I'll see you tomorrow."

She nodded, feeling warm.

"Tomorrow night," she said softly. And her body throbbed in expectation.

Chapter Five

It might be wrong of her, lying on her bed in her nightgown with her window wide open, waiting for Stephen. She was taking a terrible risk. But the heat that radiated outward from deep in the pit of her stomach told her that, after last night's encounter, she didn't care. She wanted Stephen far too much to think about the possible ramifications.

She'd lived the past ten years of her life in fear. No . . . she'd lived in fear since she was seven, when her father the king had remarried the jealous, violent actress that had tried to eliminate all competition. Beth had measured each step carefully, devoting herself to staying out of the limelight, keeping her head down, protecting herself. She'd never really gotten close to a man.

Tonight, that all was going to change.

"Beth?"

She jumped, startled. "Yes?"

Stephen climbed into her window, outlined by moonlight. "This feels so high school," he said wryly, in a low whisper. "Are you sure we aren't going to wake anybody up, staying here? Would you rather go somewhere else? Somewhere . . . more private?"

She blushed. She'd thought about going to the meadow—but that seemed to be Lydia's private terrain, and frankly, while she was interested in sex, she did not want to continue watching Lydia's all-out extravaganzas in orgiastic excess. Tonight was going to be a big enough step without that additional pressure. "Here's fine," Beth assured him hastily. "There's no one in the room next to me, and Goodmaid Amelia is in the room across. She snores loudly, and she sleeps like the dead." She paused, then let out a short, hysteria-tinged giggle, unlike her normal laugh at all. "God. That sounds so horribly unromantic."

He seemed to understand. He put his arms out, enveloping her in a hug, and kissed the top of her head. It felt warm, and comforting. However, his close proximity and the masculine scent of him gave a sensual edge to his casual gesture. "You're nervous," he stated.

She shrugged.

"Mind if we turn on the light?"

She bit her lip. "Someone might see," she said, frowning. "More people wander around at night than I'd realized."

He laughed, and she knew he was thinking of the tryst they'd watched. "That was something," he said. "You never would've suspected it, not in a little place like this. But when you get people repressed enough—well, it's bound to happen."

"You think that this—us—is just repression?" She didn't mean to sound so appalled, but she pulled away nonetheless. She wasn't sure what was between the two of them, but he had a point. She was near the breaking point, and she knew that driving, insatiable hunger was definitely a factor.

The thing is, she might have had the hunger, but she didn't have the drive until she met him.

"No. I don't understand what's between us." He sounded genuinely puzzled. Then he grinned, the lopsided, mischievous grin that made warmth curl through her chest and belly. "Mind you, I'm not complaining."

She smiled. "I'm not, either."

"Are you sure about the light? I really would love to see you."

He sounded so eager—so hopeful. She didn't want to disappoint him. She closed the shutters, then lit the lamp on her small table.

He was wearing his usual button-up shirt and trousers. His gaze took in all of her, from her hair done up in a braid down her back to her long, prim nightgown. She shifted her weight, fidgeting, and her fingers laced together.

"God, you're beautiful," he said slowly.

She smiled. "I'm not wearing anything . . . you know. Sexy."

"You don't need to." His eyes echoed his voice. "I want you."

Heat flared through her. "I know," she said.

For a second, they stood there, pulses pounding, breathing uneven. Then, in a fluid motion, they reached for each other.

He kissed her, hard, with none of the tender restraint of their encounter by the meadow. His lips covered hers with firm force, his tongue sweeping out to tangle with hers. She didn't shrink from his sensual onslaught. On the contrary, she lifted her head to meet his, her fingertips clutching at his shoulders, her pussy throbbing madly as she felt a flow of wetness rush between her thighs. She whimpered as need built with ever quickening force.

"This is crazy," he said in a ragged voice, pulling away from her.

"I know," she said. "I need you to touch me."

His eyes burned with intensity. "Any place in particular?"

"Everywhere," she said softly. She needed to feel his hands on her. She needed the pressure of his touch to somehow calm the storm that was building inside her.

He studied her, as if wondering where to begin. Then he lifted up her nightgown, pulling it over her head in one smooth motion.

She was wearing her bra and panties, which were plain white and certainly meant more for function than seduction. He still stared at her, his hands cupping the fullness of her breasts, thumbs stroking the smooth curves of skin that threatened to spill out of their containment. She arched her back, pressing more firmly into his palms, and he sighed in gratitude, leaning forward to press hot, velvety kisses against her throat.

He pulled away, and she made a small sound of protest. Before she could say anything, he tugged at the buttons of his shirt, quickly and clumsily undoing them and then tossing the garment next to her nightgown.

She stared at his chest for a moment, overwhelmed with sheer feminine appreciation of his chiseled torso. His shoulders were yoked with muscle, his chest and stomach carved in flat planes. Thin lines cut from his pelvis, arching below his waistband. She reached out tentatively, then put her palms on his chest, smoothing them down the line of his torso to his belly button. He groaned in response.

Then her hands moved lower, stroking over the fly of his pants. There was already a sizable ridge of flesh, straining against the fabric. She stroked the length of it, exploring as she hadn't been able to, last night, in their hurried encounter.

"Give me a second," he rasped. Then he unbuttoned his pants, kicking off his shoes and socks and tugging the trousers down, leaving them on the floor. He was left in boxers, his erection springing to tent the material in front of him.

She stared at the bulge, her fingers tingling in anticipation.

"There you go," he said, grinning smugly. "Now you can stroke all you like."

His voice was a teasing invitation. She felt a little self-conscious. She'd never touched a man's penis before, certainly not in the flesh, and the thin material of the boxers left little to the imagination. She started to reach forward, then pulled her hand back. "Maybe . . . we can get back to that," she said, feeling the blush heating her chest and creeping up to her face.

He nodded, his face still somewhat amused, but his eyes glowing with understanding. "We've got all night," he murmured in agreement.

"What are we going to do tonight?" she whispered.

"Whatever you want."

She shivered in anticipation. "I believe I already said I want you to touch me," she breathed.

"Believe me," he promised, "I'm going to. But it might help if you lie down."

She eyed her narrow cot, then pulled a thick quilt out of her footlocker. "I'm sorry," she said, spreading it out on the floor. "The bed's just too narrow, and you're so big."

His eyes gleamed. "No problem. This makes it like a picnic."

The way he looked at her suggested it was more than metaphorical. He looked like he wanted to eat her up.

She rubbed her thighs together. Her panties were already soaked.

He stretched out next to her, and she caught a tantalizing glimpse of his cock through the opening of his boxers. Before she could stare, he tilted her chin up, so her eyes met his. "Would you mind taking your hair out of its braid?" he said. "I'd love to see it."

She sat up, undoing the braid until her hair fell in loose waves down to her waist. He groaned, running his fingers through it. Then he rubbed her scalp. After having it secured so tightly, the pressure felt wonderful, and she purred in response.

"Do you like it when I touch you like this?" he asked.

"Yes," she admitted. "Although . . . that wasn't the touching I had in mind."

She was shocked at her own audacity. Still, he laughed, and his hands stroked her face, her earlobes, her jawline. "This better?"

"You're toying with me," she accused playfully.

"No." To her surprise, he leaned down, sucking at her nipple through the cotton of her bra. She gasped, her back arching automatically. "That's toying with you. This is just building things up a little."

"Then I want you to toy with me," she said breathlessly.

He laughed again. "Trust me. You don't want to rush this."

But she did. She thought she would go insane if something wasn't done to relieve the agonizing sexual pressure, building up inside of her. She reached behind her, forcing herself to act quickly, before she could think about it. She unhooked her bra, slipping the straps off her shoulders and tossing it aside. Then she looked at him, chin raised.

He stared at her revealed breasts, then into her eyes. "Now who's toying?" His voice was a rough velvet growl.

He leaned down, pressing kisses from her collar bone down to her breastbone. He cupped one breast with his hand. His mouth covered her nipple, sucking softly, and she let out a soft cry as pleasure shot through her, from her breast down to her cunt. Her hips raised slightly in response. He continued his gentle suckling as his hand kneaded her breast softly, his thumb circling the taut nipple, tweaking it, caressing it. Her hands threaded in his honey blond hair, holding him against her breast. She writhed as pleasure shook through her.

It wasn't enough though. She wanted more—needed more.

She let go of him, her hands venturing down the bunched tension of his arms, then to his waist . . . then to the waistband of his boxers. She took a deep breath, then let her fingertips creep past his waistband. She felt the crinkly hair beneath, and then reached lower.

He grabbed her wrist. "You're speeding things up," he said. He sounded out of breath.

She extended her fingers, feeling her index finger brush the head of his cock. She hadn't realized it would be so marvelously smooth, so satiny soft. "Is this . . . bad?" She suddenly realized she was playing a game whose rules she was completely unfamiliar with. Maybe he expected her to be pliant. He knew what he was doing, and he'd told her specifically that they needed to go slow. Was she annoying him? His face looked dark, taut with tension. She immediately withdrew her hand, guilt and embarrassment forcing back some of her desire.

He surprised her by taking her hand, then pulling down his boxers, letting his cock spring forth. It was large, a dull reddish-purple, the dark thick head capping the straight, strong length of his shaft. "You can touch, all you like," he said. "But if you keep touching me, then I'll come. And I don't want to do that just yet. I don't think you want me to, either."

She'd obviously never seen a man come before, either. She didn't know how it would affect him. Would he leave? Fall asleep? She knew how drained she'd felt after she'd shuddered her release against his palm, last night by the tree.

"I've never seen . . . one," she said, hedging, "in real life before."

He leaned back, pulling his boxers off. He lay there, beautifully naked. "What do you think?"

She studied it. "Can I touch it a little?"

His laugh sounded strangled. "Just a little," he conceded, but his eyes burned with intensity despite his smile.

She put out her hand, stroking the mushroom-shaped tip. It was a darker color, the small opening like a tiny eye in the middle, the curve of the cap splitting on the underside. There was a vein on the shaft. She traced it with her fingers. The shaft wasn't as soft as the head, but it was still smooth, and it pulsed with life. She went lower, down to where the shaft connected with his body. Beneath, his balls hung slightly, covered with hair. She rolled them over her palms, smiling slightly. The testicles felt loose, gliding easily in their sac.

He tilted his head back, and a tiny drop of clear liquid beaded on the tip of his cock. She stared at it . . . then smoothed her fingertip over it.

"God," he groaned. "Okay. Enough exploration. You'll have to give me a second to get my control back."

She smiled at the thought of being able to make a big man like this lose control with the touch of her fingertips.

He took several deep breaths, then reached for her. "Your turn."

He slipped his fingers under the elastic of her panties, slipping them down the length of her legs. She shivered under his gaze.

"Beautiful," he repeated, then his hand smoothed gently over the curves of her calf, her thigh, before reaching between her legs. His finger slid between her curls. "You're already wet for me," he said, his voice appreciative.

She bit her lip, looking away. "I get wet whenever I think of you."

He groaned, and his finger probed deeper, parting the slick folders of her pussy. He brushed past her clit, and she moaned softly, parting her legs a little more to give him better access.

"I want to look at you," he said. "It's only fair."

She wasn't sure what he meant until he sat up, parting her legs, then getting up to settle his body between them. Her breathing went shallow, her hands fisting at her sides.

"Trust me," he said.

"I do."

With that, she tilted her head back and let him start to explore.

Stephen couldn't believe what was happening. He hadn't expected to find a gorgeous woman here, on an assignment of all places. Especially not in a place that swore celibacy above all things. But here he was, sequestered in her bedroom, with this unbelievable woman lying naked and as enticing as a Christmas present, spread out in front of him, ready for the taking.

He knew he was crossing an ethical bridge, but from the moment he'd first touched her pussy, he'd tossed professionalism to the wind. Even if it meant the story—hell, right now, even if it meant his *job*—he had to have this woman. Need lashed at his body, his cock straining to get inside her wet, tight slot, feeling her cunt massage the rock-hard length of him . . .

No. Slow down. She was the inexperienced one here. He knew what he was doing, and he knew that if he buried himself in her now, he'd lose his mind, and her first experience would be quick and disappointing. And as much as he wanted her, he felt overwhelmed by the responsibility of making sure she enjoyed their sex as much as he did.

No. It was more than a responsibility. It was an *honor*. He couldn't remember if he'd ever thought of sex as an honor before.

He reached down, parting the wet folds of her flesh, pushing the ebony curls out of the way to reveal her pussy, opening like a dusky pink orchid, with the deeper rose colored flesh of her clit and inner labia curling like a tight bud. He inhaled the heady scent of her, sweet and yet spicy, like some kind of exotic island flower. He stroked the bud with his finger. Her clit was already erect, standing at attention, and liquid dripped from her like honey. He dipped a finger inside, drawing it out slowly, reveling in the sound of passion that came from her. He put his finger in his mouth. "You taste sweet," he said. "Like spice cake, but with a little tang."

She looked embarrassed, and he grinned. "You taste fantastic," he continued. "Does this feel good?"

"Yes," she breathed, her hips lifting up off the quilt to meet his probing finger. He withdrew, stroking her hard clit with slow, circular strokes. Her breathing came in quick, sharp little gasps.

With his other hand, he pressed a finger in deep, feeling her flesh tight around it. She squeezed him, and his cock jerked in anticipation of how her hot, wet cunt would feel, closing around him. He shuddered, stopping for a second, struggling with his need.

"More," she begged, her hips pressing against his hand.

He pressed a second finger in, stretching out the tight

walls of her vagina, making it easier for her to accommodate him. Her thighs closed against his wrist, holding his hand captive. His thumb continued working her clit.

"You're . . . you're going to make . . . me . . . come . . ." she forced out, panting quickly.

He smiled. "Just a second, then."

He lifted his thumb from her clit, and she let out a frustrated cry. Then he leaned forward, replacing his finger with his tongue.

She let out a tiny shriek, scooting away from him even as her hips lifted to meet his lips. Her fists clawed into the thick quilt beneath them. "Oh my God," she whispered.

He put his hands under her buttocks and curved his fingers around her hips, holding her tight to him as his teeth and tongue worked her clit. Her honey flowed over his lips and he sipped at her as his tongue moved deeper into her wet slot. She moaned, her head lolling from side to side as her body shivered beneath his ministrations.

When she stopped scooting and he felt her body start to clench, he moved one of his hands, pressing first one, then two fingers inside her, moving it gradually deeper as his tongue flicked firmly on her clit.

"*Stephen*," she gasped, her breathing coming hard and fast.

He moved his fingers in and out, searching out the spot on the high upper front of her vagina.

She cried out, and he felt her cunt milk his fingers, contracting in an undulating wave. A jolt of pre-come escaped his cock as he kept pressing inside her, drawing out the orgasm as his mouth sucked on her clit.

When it was over, he lifted his head, withdrawing his fingers, tasting them. "Spice cake," he marveled, and it described her perfectly . . . the slight heat, like ginger; the richness, like molasses; the spice, redolent of nutmeg and cinnamon and clove. "I could eat you every day."

"I don't know that I'd survive," she responded, sounding dazed. Her pupils were huge, and her pulse beat steadily in the ivory column of her throat. "But I'm perfectly willing to find out."

Her areolae were a dark pink, still jutting out against the cream of her skin. Her violet eyes were wide. She stared at him.

"Aren't you . . . don't you still . . ."

He grinned ruefully. Was she kidding? "I'm definitely not done yet," he said, the anticipation honed razor sharp in his body. He could almost come just looking at her. "I want you more than ever."

She smiled, an intoxicating mixture of demureness and seduction. "I still want you," she said. "More than ever. Especially now that I know what I have to look forward to."

He laughed, and started to reach for her. The laugh abruptly died as he thought of something.

"Did you . . . oh, shit." He closed his eyes. "What are the odds that you have a condom?"

She blinked, then blushed a rosy red. "Don't you have one?" she asked instead.

"It wasn't like they let me keep my wallet," he said. "Hell. It's not like I even keep a condom in my wallet anymore, anyway."

Her look of understanding was tragicomic. He felt sure

that he'd find it hysterical . . . some time in the distant future, after he actually had a fucking condom and he'd buried himself hip-deep in her welcoming pussy, enjoying the snug cunt he'd so thoroughly warmed with his tongue. But he couldn't laugh, not now.

It was one thing to be ethically questionable, sleeping with the subject of a potential newspaper article. But getting one pregnant . . . well, that was an entirely different issue, and not one he was willing to risk.

"Is there anything I can do?" she asked, in a small voice.

He rolled away from her, lying flat on the floor. "Unless you know of a convenience store nearby . . ." he joked, tension still slicing through his words.

She leaned over him, strands of her long ebony hair stroking over his erection, and he hissed with pleasure as the cool silk tickled at him. She pushed the wayward locks out of the way. "Can't I do for you," she whispered, "what you did for me?"

He stared at her. "It's your first time," he protested. "I can't ask you. You don't know what you'd be in for."

"You worried you'd come if I touched you," she said, her soft palm reaching forward and circling the hard base of his cock. "You don't need to worry about that now."

He didn't trust himself to speak, so he stayed silent. She tugged at the flesh of his cock gently, stroking him inexpertly, but getting him worked up nonetheless. He didn't have far to go.

She leaned over him, her breasts round and firm, her raspberry lips pursed. She cupped him with both hands, stroking him.

"It would help . . . if we had a little lubricant," he admitted.

She smiled. "Would this help?"

With that, her head tipped down, and she took the head of his cock into her mouth.

He let out a guttural groan of pleasure as she suckled his cock gently. Her mouth wasn't very big, and he felt the sharp edge of her teeth graze against the head, but with deliberate gentleness. The startling sensation almost sent him over the edge, and like she had when she was the one on her back, his hands fisted into the quilt below him. He thought he might rip it apart as the pressure inside him increased, causing all his muscles to tense. His hips raised, and he couldn't help it . . . he pressed his cock a little further into the welcoming warmth of her mouth, with her curious, catlike tongue and moist full lips. She let some saliva run down his shaft on to her hands, then stroked with increasing firmness, as if gaining confidence.

The sensation was more than he could bear.

"Beth . . . honey, I'm gonna come," he grunted, nudging her away, but she held firm, her lips clamping around his cock. He couldn't hold back any more. He let go, the orgasm shooting from him, into her waiting mouth. She kept sucking at him, and to his shock, a second round of shudders rocked him.

He might be mistaken, but he might have had a multiple. *How the* hell *did that happen?*

He had difficulty breathing, so he simply lay back, struggling to regain his wind. She kept on him, licking at him, suckling him until he started to go limp. Then she kissed each of his balls before looking at him. Her smile reminded him of the Mona Lisa . . . small, mysterious. She kissed his stomach, then moved up to his chest before lying next to him.

"I'm sorry," he said. "I tried to warn you, but . . ."

"It's all right," she said, pressing a small, endearing kiss on his shoulder.

"That was your first time," he protested. "That had to be . . . well, not what you were expecting."

Her smile broadened. "You know . . . you don't taste like spice cake."

He winced. "I'll bet."

"This isn't going to sound romantic," she said, actually sounding studious, "but you reminded me of . . . well, clam chowder. Sort of salty."

He stared at her. Then he laughed, a low, delighted sound. "I really like you, Beth."

Her answering smile was like the sun coming out from behind a cloud.

"I like you, too," she said. "And I'd like to do this again sometime." She looked at him from below the thick fringe of her lashes.

"We'll have to work on that," he said, smiling. "This, and more."

Chapter Six

Beth knocked softly on the door to Lydia's room. It was after the waking bell, but not quite time for breakfast. There was nothing in the rules that said she simply couldn't talk to another woman, but considering her purpose in the early morning visit, she still felt her heart speeding up irrationally.

Lydia opened the door, her red hair tumbling around her shoulders, her dress half buttoned. "Yes?" she asked, her voice thick with sleep.

Beth glanced up and down the hall. "I need to talk to you."

Lydia recognized her, and all traces of sleep vanished from her features, replaced with an alert caution. She motioned Beth in.

Lydia's room was neat as a pin, nothing out of place. Beth wondered if she'd ever had a "guest" here in the women's dormitory. Beth suspected not. Lydia kept up an immaculate front.

"Why are you here?"

Beth took a deep breath, steeling herself. "I want one of the condoms the delivery woman gave me yesterday."

Lydia stared at her for a moment, then a slow, wicked smile spread across her face. *"Really."*

Beth felt the blush creep up her chest, but forged ahead. "Yes."

"Take two . . . I've got plenty." Lydia stuck a chair under her door, jamming it shut. Then she pulled up a floorboard, next to the foot of her bed. She pulled out the foil packages, handing it to Beth with a flourish. "Anyone I know?"

It took Beth a second to realize what Lydia was asking. The heat of the blush grew more intense.

"It's not your business," Beth said curtly.

"No," Lydia agreed, her eyes going hard. "But what happened in the meadow wasn't your business, and neither was my arrangement with the delivery woman, but you managed to stick your nose in that."

Beth felt a twinge of guilt. "You weren't exactly private about it," she said. "It wasn't my fault I saw what I saw, or overheard what I did."

"Fine," Lydia said, shrugging, but Beth could tell she was still annoyed. "I guess you've been having sex and keeping it under wraps for ages—you've been here, what, ten years? Have you just been barebacking it all this time?"

Beth took a step back, bewildered. "I don't understand."

Lydia stared at her. "You really don't, do you?" she said, and her voice was tinged with condescension. She replaced the board in the floor, then went about arranging her hair and pulling on her veil. "Good grief. How old are you?"

"What does that have to do with anything?" Beth felt distinctly uncomfortable. The condoms felt conspicuous, even hidden in her pocket. Her fingertips slid over the smooth packaging.

"You can't possibly still be a virgin, can you?"

"Why does everyone ask that?" Beth groused. "There are virgins even on the outside, you know. Even *normal* people."

Lydia scoffed. "Are you kidding? Do you know how rare a virgin is these days? Like a unicorn or a mermaid or some other mythic creature. Virgins are something out of fairy tales, Beth."

Beth stared at her as she watched Lydia transform into her perfect Penitent facade. "What are you doing here?" Beth asked.

Lydia shrugged. "My family sent me here," she said finally. "I was on an Amish commune, but I managed to go to a public school. I realized that there was a whole world I was missing. So I made up for it." She shrugged delicately. "I wound up experimenting with a few of the boys on the commune . . . and one of the girls. They thought I was wicked and needed more discipline. My father is friends with Founder Roberts, and he arranged for me to be sent here."

Beth was aghast. "Against your will?" She might have been happy here, but she had come willingly—and the place was a paradise, compared with her life at the palace. If she had been forced . . .

She realized that it was not necessarily something she would have chosen. She frowned at the thought.

Lydia's laugh was brittle. "What other choice did I have?"

"You could have . . . I don't know. Told him that you wouldn't go. Stood up to him."

"You don't want to know what he would have done to me if I did." Lydia's face went dark.

Beth swallowed hard. "All right. You could have run away."

"Do you know how hard it is out there?" Lydia said derisively. "No. I understand communes . . . how they work, what the system is. And I'm more careful here. I can do whatever I want, as long as I'm careful." She winked at Beth, her mischievous expression at odds with the sternness of her outfit. "You can, too. With as many people as you want . . . as long as they're careful."

"It's not like that," Beth stammered. "There's . . . there's just one."

"Oh." Lydia rolled her eyes as she moved the chair from under the door handle. "I guess you're going to tell me you're in love."

Beth blinked. "I don't know," she whispered, feeling her stomach clench in a knot. "I've never been in love."

"Well, even if he's mentioned love, men will say anything to get sex." Lydia sounded definitive. "I learned that on the outside. And even in a place like this, it's still true. They'll say anything if they think they can get some action."

"He hasn't mentioned love."

Lydia's eyes widened. "Well, at least he's honest," she said. "Huh. Well, if he knows you're a virgin, then he probably won't mind if you're clumsy and inexperienced. You, on the other hand . . . I guess you're just in it for the sex, then."

Beth straightened. She hadn't thought about it that way, and now that Lydia had put it in that context . . . she frowned with distaste.

"I wouldn't have guessed it," Lydia said, with a small smile. "No matter what anybody else said, I figured you for a good girl."

"What are people saying?" Beth asked, shocked even further.

"Oh, you know." Lydia opened the door, and the two of them started to walk down the empty hallway. "Nobody who looks like you could possibly be pure, you're running away from your past . . . that kind of thing."

Beth bit her lip. They were right about her past, at least. "They don't know what they're talking about."

"Oh, I figured," Lydia said, giving Beth an assessing glance. "But I see you've got even more secrets than I do."

Beth didn't say anything. They stepped out into the morning sunlight, joining the women filing toward the Dining Hall to prepare breakfast.

"If you need anything else," Lydia said, her voice deceptively mild, "I meet with the delivery woman every Thursday. You can place an order, if you like."

The blush returned.

"And do let me know if you need any pointers," Lydia added, her expression placid as she nodded good morning to the other women. "It's the Penitent way for women to be helpful, as you know."

Beth turned away, going to the refrigerator to try and cool her face down. The nerve of the woman, she thought bitterly. Offering to give her pointers. Telling her she's just in it for the sex. Who did Lydia think she was?

Of course, it did bring up the question . . . why *was* Beth doing all this?

She thought of Stephen. His green eyes, his smile, his body.

Was it all purely physical? And if it was . . . was that really what she wanted to risk her future, possibly even her life, for?

"Are you here just to have sex with me?"

Stephen stopped in the act of climbing in Beth's darkened window. Her voice emerged from the shadows, and he was unable to make out her form. "Uh . . . no."

"What else would you be here for?"

He made it in the rest of the way, stepping into the dark and closing the window behind him, snapping the shutters tightly. The room was pitch-black and stifling. "Could we turn on the light before we discuss this?" he said, reaching out blindly.

He heard her sigh, then the light came on, momentarily blinding him. As his eyes adjusted, he saw her standing next to her table, her feet bare, her nightgown on, buttoned primly. Her hair was loose, hanging down past her shoulders, covering her breasts and tumbling to her waist. She looked beautiful, as always, but her eyes looked wary.

"What's this about, Beth?"

She walked over to the bed, sitting down and tucking her knees up to her chest, covered in the skirt of the nightgown.

She looked younger than her years, and vulnerable. "I got a condom," she said.

His dick, already at half-mast, started to spring to full life. "How?"

"It doesn't matter," she said, hugging her knees. "It occurred to me: I'm taking a big risk here. I could get thrown out—banished—if they discovered us. And I wondered why I'm doing this."

He gritted his teeth. Hormones were flooding his system, like a car engine revving too high, and in the front of his mind the thought of the way she'd enthusiastically sucked on his cock the night before only pushed him to a fever pitch. But now she was having recriminations. Buyer's remorse. "You don't have anything to feel guilty about, Beth. There's nothing wrong with what we did."

"Why do I react this way to you?" she asked, rocking slightly. "Whenever I see you, I feel like . . . like there's nothing else that matters. Is it just physical? Chemical? Have I just lost my mind?"

He sat on the bed next to her, putting his arm around her shoulders and squeezing comfortingly. "You affect me, too," he said.

"You're a man," she replied, her tone dismissive.

"I've turned down enough women to know this isn't a normal reaction," he said sharply. "Don't lump me in with all the other horn dogs you might've known. I wasn't a monk before I met you, but I've got restraint. And I can tell you this: what's going on between us is special."

She stared at him, her eyes wide. "Is it . . ." She swallowed. "It's not love, is it?"

She sounded cautious, but hopeful.

He closed his eyes. She was a virgin, he reminded himself. Despite her age, she was still innocent enough to believe, or want to believe, in love. "I don't know," he hedged.

She seemed to go very still. "I see," she said. Her voice was very small.

He felt like a bastard. "We barely know each other," he pointed out, trying to justify his cruelty. "I think love takes years. You know."

"So you've never been in love, either?"

He sighed. "I thought I was," he admitted. "Then she slept with another man, and . . . well. I figured out I was just naive."

"I'm sorry," Beth said, leaning against him, and while he figured he'd buried the emotion from that episode years ago, he was surprised how fresh the sting was—and how much Beth's warmth was a comforting balm against the feelings. "You must have been devastated."

"It hurt. But I got over it," he said. "You've never been in love?"

She shook her head. "I knew a man . . . I was interested in him," she said.

Stephen felt a spurt of jealousy shoot through him. "What happened?"

"He died."

She'd had a hell of a life, wherever she'd lived before here. He didn't feel sorry for her. She didn't paint herself as a victim. She just kept plowing forward, doing what needed to be done, enjoying the little life she'd carved out for herself here.

"It's not just sex," he found himself saying. "I don't know what else it is—but it's more than physical, Beth."

She studied his face, her violet eyes soul-searching. Slowly, she nodded.

"I know," she agreed. "Whatever it is . . . I'm glad it's you."

Stephen felt his chest warm with a glowing, expansive feeling, something he wasn't familiar with. He suddenly felt larger than life, heroic, like Sir Lancelot and Spiderman rolled into one. He stroked her hair.

"We won't do anything you're not comfortable with," he said. He didn't care what his body needed. This woman was special . . . and this wasn't just sex.

"You make me feel comfortable," she said softly. "You make me feel . . . wonderful."

"Sweetie," he said, "you ain't seen nothin' yet."

He got the quilt out, laying it carefully on the floor, then lifted her off of the bed. She weighed next to nothing, and he placed her carefully on the quilt, nuzzling the top of her head with his chin. She let out a tiny laugh.

He needed her to see how wonderful she was, and how different what he was feeling was. When she reluctantly reached for her nightgown, starting to tug it over her head, he stopped her.

"There's no rush," he said. "Let's just sit a minute."

She looked puzzled. Then he leaned in, kissing her softly, rubbing his lips over the velvety softness of her mouth.

He breathed in her sigh, and she melted against him. He crushed the satiny mass of her hair in his hand, holding her head to his, tantalizing her tongue with his own. Her breathing sped up, and he moved his mouth, kissing her cheeks, her eyelids, causing her to giggle girlishly. Her laugh turned into a small gasp as he nipped at her earlobe, then sucked at it gently. She leaned against him, hard.

"Like that, do you?" he whispered in her ear, his voice breathy and soft.

"*Mmmmm.*" She rubbed against him, like a cat.

He stroked her hair out of the way, kissing the nape of her neck, and the spot between her shoulder blades that was exposed by her neckline.

"Stephen," she breathed, turning. Then, slowly, she unbuttoned one, then another of the buttons down the front of her gown, exposing the cleavage between her breasts.

He nuzzled between them, his tongue lightly stroking the shadowed cleft between each breast, and her breathing sped up.

"You always know how to touch me." Her voice sounded appreciative.

"How are you feeling?" he asked, concerned. "Because I could do this all night."

She looked at him with wide violet eyes, her expression solemn. "I'm ready," she said.

He sighed, studying her. "Not by a long shot," he said. "But I'll get you there."

She stared, puzzled. He shook his head. He couldn't explain it to her . . . but he could show her.

Slowly, he stripped out of his clothes, the feel of her gaze hungrily covering every inch of him like a burning trail over his skin. His cock jutted out, heavy and dark. When she did that tiny lip-lick with her pointed tongue, he groaned, a drop of pre-come beading on the head. She reached out, smoothing the drop over his skin. He leaned forward in response. His muscles felt like corded iron.

Rein it in, he chastised himself. She might be curious, but she was still nervous, and this was still about her. It was all about her.

"You have that condom?"

She nodded, getting up, her hair tumbling exotically as she grabbed it from the pocket of her day dress. She dropped the packet on the quilt. Then, biting her lip, she tugged the nightgown over her head.

He meant to stop her. He wanted to take it slowly, easing the garment off of her with heated kisses and gentle strokes. But what he saw took his breath away.

She wasn't wearing any underwear. Her breasts were high and firm, her waist narrow, flaring into generous hips. The ebony thatch of hair covering her cunt curled invitingly at the juncture of the pale skin of her thighs. She knelt down on the quilt, looking determined.

"Remember last night?" he asked, his voice strained.

Her look of determination eased, and she smiled slowly. "Yes."

He smiled, his voice full of tenderness . . . and promise.

"This is going to be better."

Beth watched as he stretched out naked beside her. Her skin was ultra-sensitive, her nipples already erect, her body covered in goose bumps despite the heat.

She ought to feel guiltier. She'd been stewing about the possible ramifications of tonight all day, since her talk with Lydia. But now, with him in the small confines of her room, his naked body beckoning to her, she felt all her inhibitions falling away as she succumbed to the hunger that he always brought out in her.

Maybe it is just sex. But whatever it is, it's magical.

He kissed her, slow, drugging kisses with his lips and tongue, and she parted her lips willingly. His fingertips smoothed over her, leaving no inch untouched. He stroked the delicate skin at the inner crook of her elbows; he caressed the under curve beneath her breasts, hovering at her rib cage. He kissed her waist and hips. His palms massaged her in long, lazy glides, slowly rubbing her skin to life, causing it to tingle with warmth. Her pussy, which had been damp, grew wet with a gradual progression. It was different than the fervent build-up of the night before. That had been an inferno of need, stymied by their lack of protection. This was gentle, persistent . . . and consequently, it built the flames even higher. She arched her back as he took first one, then the other breast into his mouth, suckling her thoroughly as he stroked her hips, letting the hot, blunt tip of his cock drag over her stomach, or slide intriguingly between her thighs, stopping just short of her cunt. Each time it got close, she held her breath. She began to suspect that his teasing was deliberate, since he was always doing something somewhere else to distract her. Finally, she cuddled the hard length of him between her thighs.

"I want to feel you," she gasped.

He shook his head. "Not yet," he said, his voice strained. "You're not quite ready yet."

"I'm ready," she protested. Her pussy was practically dripping with need, and she spread her legs, arching her pelvis up. She felt the broad head of his cock press against her, and a jolt of sensation shot through her. She whimpered, trying to push him deeper.

He groaned and pulled away. "This is your first time," he said. "I don't want to hurt you."

"But I need you . . ."

"Wait for me," he said. Then he leaned down, pressing his fingers into her curls, parting the lips of her vagina. Her clit was hard, and he pressed his thumb against it. She cried out, then started panting as he pressed a finger inside her. "You're so wet. So tight."

She gritted her teeth, grinding her hips against his hand.

"I want you to come, baby," he said. "This way, first. It'll make it easier."

Make what easier? She was getting lost, confused by the sensations roiling through her. His mouth covered her, and he started to suck on her clit as another finger pressed into her pussy.

She shrieked softly as an orgasm shot through her, quick and hard as a gunshot. Her body, remembering last night, had built up too much anticipation, and the orgasm was a sharp echo of the night before. He pulled his mouth away, watching her as she got her bearings.

"Better?" he asked.

She nodded, breathing hard. "But . . . it's not quite . . . enough."

"I'm going to get you ready," he said, leaning his mouth close to her ear. "Then, slowly, I'm going to put my cock inside you. And you're going to tell me how it feels. I want to make sure it feels good."

She nodded, shivering at the caress of his voice.

"Does talk like that shock you?"

"No," she replied.

"Do you like it?"

She bit her lip. "Yes," she admitted.

She could hear the smile in his voice. "Would you like to try it?"

She suddenly remembered when she'd watched Lydia and Henry, that first night in the meadow. *I've wanted your cock all week,* Lydia had said, without a second's hesitation.

"I . . . ," Beth started, then stopped, too embarrassed.

"Don't worry," Stephen reassured her. "Don't worry about anything."

And strangely, Beth didn't. She just went along for the ride.

And what a ride it is.

He opened the foil package, producing the thin, flexible condom. She watched as he rolled it on the hard length of his erection. Then he stroked her pussy, now slick-wet with her come. He put two fingers inside again, slowly, and she took a deep breath as his fingers spread, widening her. She moved her hips against his hand.

"Eager," he said with approval, kissing the side of her breast.

"I want to touch you," she said.

She reached down, cupping his balls first, then gently stroking along his shaft. The condom felt funny. It was thin and slippery, sliding over his cock like a second skin.

"Easy," he said. "Don't want it to come off, now."

"Isn't that uncomfortable?"

"It's not perfect," he admitted. "And it would definitely be better if I could be inside you, naked." He sighed. "Maybe someday, we'll be able to try it. But for now, this is the best we can do."

She gasped as his fingers slowly withdrew, and he positioned himself between her thighs. She looked up at him, feeling trust and nerves warring with each other.

She felt the hard length of him, nuzzling between her thighs, before probing at the entrance of her wet cunt. She held her breath as he slowly pushed in, inch by tantalizing inch . . . until he was buried completely inside her. She felt like she was stretching to accommodate him: like her body cushioned him, like his cock fit her in a snug, perfect fit.

"Are you all right?" Sweat beaded on his forehead, and the muscles in his arms bunched. His eyes were filled with concern.

"Yes," she breathed, as she flexed experimentally, shifting her hips to feel his cock deep inside her. "Oh yes . . ."

"God, Beth," he said, his eyes closing. "You feel so fucking *good*. . . ."

She moved again, feeling his blunt cock head moving against her special spot, and she cried out.

"Are you . . ."

"There," she interrupted, swiveling her hips again so she could feel him brush against her. "Oh, Stephen, right *there* . . ."

He groaned, pulling out, and she whimpered in protest, twining her legs around his.

"Baby, you're gonna make me lose control . . ."

Embarrassment, inhibition all burned away under the

fierce intensity of her passion. "Fuck me," she said bluntly, moving her legs up to wrap around his waist. "I want to feel your cock inside me . . ."

He started moving faster inside her, harder, and she clung to him, her hips meeting his every rough thrust. His shaft dragged along her clit, and she gasped and dug her fingernails into the small of his back, pulling her to him as he slammed into her spot. The orgasm exploded through her, starting in her cunt and radiating outward, then echoing from her clit through the rest of her body. She let out a rippling cry, her entire body contracting around him.

He let out a low shout of satisfaction in the crook of her neck, muffled by her hair, as his body jerked and emptied itself in the throes of release. She still pushed to meet every shuddering motion of his hips, reveling in the feel of him inside her.

When it was over, she lay back, sweaty and dazed. She'd gratified herself before, but this . . . this was unlike anything she'd ever felt. She felt amazed, and irrepressible. She felt un-believable.

She leaned up, pressing the tiniest kiss on his neck. "Thank you."

He looked in her eyes. "It was my pleasure," he said, his deep voice rumbling through his chest. "Trust me."

She felt warmth bubble through her. He sounded like he really meant it.

"If we had another condom," he said, "I'd show you just how much pleasure it was."

Slowly, she smiled. "Actually . . . I've got one more."

* * *

He didn't know how it was possible. Even without experience, even on a quilt-covered pine board floor, this woman had managed to rock his world. The traces of vulnerability slowly moving into confidence . . . the way she'd shifted from cautious to uninhibited . . . the surprise dirty talk, hitting him like a sexual left hook . . . the way she'd clung to him, her legs wrapping around him as if she couldn't bear to let go, taking him in fully and begging for more. He'd lost himself in her, plowing into her, letting go in a complete blackout of release. Now, breathless, he only hoped he hadn't hurt her. But she'd kissed him. Hell . . . she'd *thanked* him.

And now, with her slow, wicked little smile, she was telling him she had one more condom.

His slowly deflating cock jumped up like a well-trained dog, panting and eager to get back at it. He hadn't had that quick a recovery time since college, for Christ's sake.

What is it about this woman? Of course, he wasn't complaining. He just wondered how he was going to ever be able to walk away when the story was over.

Don't think about that now.

"Another condom, you say?" he asked, with an answering smile.

She bit her lip, surveying him under thick ebony lashes. Then she nodded, her eyes gleaming violet-blue and mischievous.

"I'm obviously up for it," he said, nodding down at his bobbing cock, "if you are."

"Oh," she said, getting up on her knees, her breasts hovering over him. "I think I can be persuaded."

She turned to get the other condom, and he gave her a playful swat on her backside. She gasped, turning to him with a look of mock severity. "You'll pay for that one."

"Really?" He stretched out. "Looking forward to it." He leaned back, putting his hands behind his head, the picture of relaxation except for his cock standing up like a denuded flagpole.

She grinned back at him, holding out the condom package.

"It's all you," he said, surveying her from half-lidded eyes.

She blinked in surprise, then looked at his cock appraisingly.

"I'll talk you through it," he added, curious to see what she'd do.

It took her a minute to rip through the foil; then she had the condom unrolling the wrong way for a second. Soon, though, she had it prepped and ready for his cock.

"Let's just make sure you're ready for this," she teased, and then brushed those long, soft fingers over his rigid flesh.

He sighed as the fingers closed around him, tugging on him slightly, stroking him to an even harder state of readiness, if that was possible. Then she cupped his balls, tickling the spot just beneath in a way that drove him mad. How did she instinctively know what to do to turn him on? Or did it even matter, because no matter *what* this woman did, she turned him on?

"All right, enough playing," he growled.

She laughed, a delighted, free sound. Then she put the condom on, carefully unrolling it until it covered the length of him, right down to the base of his shaft. He stretched the tip slightly. "How do you want it," he murmured, thinking hungrily about the endless possibilities . . . and trying to keep in mind that she was still new to this, to pleasure.

"I think I want to take you this time," she said, and she blushed from her breasts to her cheeks.

He couldn't remember the last time he'd seen a woman blush as much, or as beautifully, as Beth did. "All right," he agreed easily.

She smiled. Then she straddled him.

"Wait a second," he said, "are you sure you're—"

But before he could stop to ensure she was ready for him, she impaled herself on his hard cock, her taut pussy stretching to accommodate him. He groaned at the sheer pleasure of her snug snatch fisting around his penis, and he felt a surge of pleasure rip through him like a bolt of lightning.

"Oh," she murmured, sitting still.

"Are you . . . all right?" he asked through gritted teeth.

"*Mmmm,*" she said, closing her eyes and leaning back slightly. The pressure made him dizzy with arousal. She lifted herself up, and it was all he could do not to grab her hips and drag her back over him, burying himself in her. But this was her moment—she could do what she liked. For as long as she liked.

The sheer sexual torture might kill him, but he'd die with a smile on his face.

She lowered herself down by inches, her hips pivoting slightly, rolling around him before taking him in all the way to his balls. He could feel her opening squeeze around the base of his cock, and it was almost enough to send him over the edge. He contracted his muscles, making sure that he brushed against her G-spot. She gasped, and he felt her clench around him. He bunched his jaw, his hands making fists in the quilt.

"This feels good," she breathed. "You feel good."

"You feel incredible," he echoed, his hips lifting to help his cock delve more deeply inside her.

"But I don't get to feel as much of you this way," she said, rocking against him and causing another wave of pleasure.

He closed his eyes, forcing himself to retain control. Then he said, "why don't you stretch out over me?"

She did, her breasts crushing against his chest, her hair framing their faces, her legs stretched out over his. It brought her thighs close, and her already tight cunt squeezed him even harder. "Oh," she panted, moving experimentally against him. "I like this."

He thought she might. It gave his cock even more direct friction against her erect clit. He reached down, bunching his fingers into her buttocks, cupping them against him and rubbing her up and down.

She gasped, tightening her legs together, and he moaned softly.

Beth started to move, sliding along him, their bodies moving sinuously together as his cock glided in and out of her wet, tight pussy. Her breathing grew rapid and uneven, punctuated by short, sharp gasps of pleasure. Her nipples dragged against his chest, and his cock felt ready to explode.

"Beth, baby, I'm going to come soon," he said, fighting for control. He'd just had an orgasm . . . he should've lasted much longer, but this amazing woman was driving him out of his mind.

"Stephen," she hissed, and he felt her body clench around his, hard and sharp. *"Stephen!"*

She shuddered against him, her flesh shivering against his, and he let go, thrusting into her, his cock sliding home as the orgasm shot through him, draining him.

After long moments, he leaned up, kissing her softly and tenderly on the lips, stroking her hair away from her face.

"Thank *you*," he said, answering the puzzled expression on her face. "It's never been like this for me before."

Her face softened. "Really?"

"Really."

She rolled off of him, then rolled again, stretching out on her stomach and looking at him with a wide, clear smile of pure pleasure. That heroic feeling ran through him again.

I'm never going to get enough of this . . .

His thought stopped in its tracks as he noticed a dark spot, high up on her left buttock, close to the small of her back. "I bruised you."

Her eyes widened, and she flipped away from him. "No, no. I'm fine."

Guilt assailed him. "Let me see," he said, gently turning her. "That looks bad."

"No," she said. "Really. It's just a birthmark."

He glanced. Sure enough, it was a café-au–lait-colored patch of skin. "That's funny," he said. "It looks like an apple . . ."

Suddenly, his mouth snapped shut as his brain, which had apparently taken a vacation since he'd laid eyes on Beth, finally put all the pieces of the puzzle together.

"Black hair. Blue eyes. Twenty-seven years old," he muttered, staring at her. *"Apple shaped birthmark on the small of your back."*

The color drained out of her face, and she grabbed her nightgown, pulling it haphazardly over her head.

He waited for her face to reemerge. "Holy shit," he whispered. "You're . . . Princess Bianca. The one everybody thinks is dead."

He reached for her, but she pulled away from him like he was the devil. "I didn't want you to know," she said. "Nobody's supposed to know."

"But we need to talk about this," he said, his mind reeling. "I'm a reporter, and—"

"You're a *what?*"

He winced. He probably could've picked a better time to mention that little detail. "I'm a reporter. But it's not what you—"

She hit the light, then threw open the shutter and bolted out the window. He cursed, trying to find his pants in the dark. He wasn't going to run after her naked. By the time he got his pants back on, she was long gone.

He waited for her until close to sunrise, then he grabbed his things, retreating back to the men's dormitory before he was missed. He couldn't afford to get banished, not now.

Not when he'd just had incredible sex with a woman the world had been obsessed with for ten long years.

Chapter Seven

Three days later, Beth rubbed at her eyes, peering out through the slats in her shutters. The sky was turning the peculiar shade of colorless gray that signaled sunrise wasn't far off. She put it at maybe four thirty in the morning.

She kept the windows shut and barred every night, now. Stephen had come every night, whispering.

Beth . . . Beth, you have to listen to me.

I didn't mean to trick you. I'd never hurt you.

You've got to believe me.

Please. Open up.

She'd covered her head with her pillow, pretending she couldn't hear him.

She didn't know what was worse: that he now knew who she was, or that *she* now knew who *he* was.

A reporter. A goddamned reporter, here, in the sanctuary

she'd counted on for the past ten years. Her sense of safety was shattered.

She wondered if the betrayal would have been so devastating if he hadn't just introduced her to the most intense pleasure her body had ever known. Her pussy throbbed at the mere thought of him. She'd caught glimpses of him, during mealtimes, and though she'd forced herself not to meet his gaze, she could feel his glance roaming over her like a physical touch. Her nipples would go hard and pointed, and she would shift restlessly in her seat, her thighs rubbing together, feeling the dampness lubricating them in anticipation of his touch.

She wanted him. Even knowing that he would ruin everything, that he'd no doubt willingly endanger her life for a few square inches of print . . . she still wanted him.

She didn't know what to do about any of it. He had no proof, other than her birthmark. He had no witnesses, no photos. But if he were resourceful, he'd find a way, and then she'd be at his mercy.

Maybe you could trust him.

She heard a small, bitter laugh, and realized she'd made the sound. Trust? A reporter?

You trusted him with your body.

She closed her eyes. Ah, but that was different. Her body had trusted him. It still trusted him.

Her body had its own agenda.

She grabbed her towel. She'd go to the women's bathing house, take a long shower. There would still be hot water, before all the other women awoke, and she'd get some precious time alone to come up with some kind of solution. She knew she couldn't avoid Stephen forever, and she was running out of options.

Stephen was just about to head back to the men's dormitory when he saw her leaving her building. He'd kept watch every night for the past three days, trying to get a chance to talk to her . . . trying to get her alone.

The Princess.

She was a tabloid's wet dream. Born of an Oscar-winning actress and the king of a small but wealthy island nation in the South Pacific, Princess Bianca Cordova had everything going for her: looks, money, royal blood. Tragedy struck when she was seven: her mother died of cancer, and the world mourned with her. She became even more of a legend.

Then the king remarried. He'd had so much luck with actresses the first time, he'd tried again, but without as much success. Rumors had it he was going to divorce Bianca's stepmother, Andrea, for her wild partying, careless spending, and continual cosmetic enhancements, but he died of a heart attack before he could file the paperwork. Paparazzi followed the young Princess at her boarding schools, chronicling her hereditary beauty, and speculated about the future when she finally assumed the throne. When she "died" at seventeen, nobody wanted to believe it. Hell, nobody *did* believe it. The tabloid press had a field day. Sightings of her were everywhere. True nutcases had even claimed that they'd seen her with Elvis: *The Princess runs off with "the King."* It was madness.

But after a few years, people began to believe the girl really had died. After all, with a face that famous, there was no place on earth that she could hide, right?

He grimaced. *Wrong.*

And he had the exclusive story. He couldn't believe his luck. It was like being assigned to the world's crappiest, most fluff feature piece, the journalistic equivalent of a pie-eating contest . . . and then discovering Jimmy Hoffa's body under the contest table. He'd unwittingly scored the big time. The brass ring? Try the twenty-four-carat-gold one.

But he wasn't stalking her because she was the biggest story of his life, although she would be. He was stalking her because he wanted . . . no. He *needed* to talk to her.

He was going crazy not seeing her. Not *touching* her.

He followed her from a safe distance. He couldn't believe he was letting sex jeopardize his career, but as he'd already told her: it was more than sex. More than he could believe, or even understand. But he had to convince her that her secret was safe with him. If she was okay with him sharing it with the world, then great, but he'd never do anything to hurt her.

Even though he really hadn't given her any reason to, it still stung that she couldn't believe that.

She had a rough gray towel slung over her shoulder, he noticed, and she was heading for the women's bathing house.

His cock, in a permanent state of semi-erection, went fully rigid. She was about to be naked, water sluicing over those glorious curves . . .

He carefully scouted around. She was up early—no one else was awake yet, it seemed. It was still pretty dark out.

He circled the side of the bathhouse. They had windows, high up on the wall, but the building was set against a sloped hill that made accessing the windows relatively easy. They weren't expecting snoopers. They certainly weren't expecting men to break in, he assumed.

He'd probably be in a world of punishment if they knew that he was invading the women's bathing house, but considering sex was probably the biggest taboo and he'd already broken that, he didn't mind adding to his list of crimes.

He crept in, landing on the tile floor. He could hear the solitary shower running, the splashing rush, steam billowing out from the tiled room. The fluorescent bulb flickered dimly over the sink and mirror, but not in the bathing area itself. He glanced inside.

She didn't hear him over the shower. In any case, she was far too occupied to notice much of anything.

She stood, gloriously naked, her body arched back as the water cascaded over that glorious long black hair of hers. Her breasts stood at attention, high and round, her nipples peaking with an erectness that had nothing to do with the cool morning air. She was leaning against the gray-blue tiles of the bathing room, under the last shower nozzle.

He watched, mesmerized, as her hand smoothed water down her shoulder, then she cupped her own breast, plumping it, pinching the nipple lightly between her thumb and forefinger. She bit her lip as her other hand slid down the smooth expanse of her stomach, inching toward the dark thatch of curls that covered her pussy. She spread her legs, her long fingers delving deeper, parting the folds of flesh. He saw a wink of pink as she exposed her labia, then her fingers nestled against her clit, hiding the delicate flesh. She let out a long, slow sigh.

He couldn't take it. Quietly, he stripped out of his clothes, getting a condom out of his pocket. He was lucky they'd assigned him to outside duty, working in the mines: they had a condom machine in the restroom there, he'd learned, and he'd quickly purchased a couple. He'd been carrying this one around like a hopeful schoolboy, living the motto Be Prepared. Now, he was glad he'd been so forward thinking.

He slipped the condom on, and crept forward silently.

He covered her mouth with his hand, stifling the scream as he interrupted her ministrations. Her eyes flew open.

"You wouldn't see me," he said, kissing her neck. "I had to see you."

She bit his hand. He yanked it away.

"You have no right," she growled, trying to get away from him, but he trapped her against the tiles, his hard, naked body getting covered in the hot water. Wet and slippery, his body slid against hers, her nipples dragging against his chest. His cock probed at her stomach, and he groaned.

"I know. I'm sorry," he breathed. "I just need you to listen to me. I wanted to tell you how sorry I am . . ."

"You're naked," she interrupted, as if she'd just realized their situation. "Oh, God, if they catch us . . ."

But her voice was breathless, and he felt her hand tentatively touch his chest . . . moving lower. Caressing the hard length of him.

"I'm so sorry," he said. "I just . . . I can't believe how much I want you. I've been going insane with it . . ."

"Me, too," she admitted softly. "We can't . . . we'll get caught . . ."

"Just a little," he murmured, his body long past caring about any repercussions. He lifted her up, her legs going easily around his waist. Her breathing had gone shallow, her pupils dilating until her blue eyes looked almost pure black. His cock pressed against her, and her hand moved down quickly, positioning him at the entrance of her pussy. He slid in, and the firm clutch of her cunt squeezing him as he entered her was mind-blowing. "Christ, that feels so fucking *good.*"

"*Aahh,*" she said, leaning her head back against the tiles and wrapping her legs around his waist, taking him in even deeper. She rocked her hips. He leaned down, water covering his face as he licked at her breasts. She twined her fingers in his hair, gently bouncing up and down. He rocked into her, his cock pressing deeper and deeper, withdrawing and then pressing forward with high, hard strokes. He reached between them, stroking at her clit. "Were you in here, thinking of me?" he asked, as he caressed the hard button of flesh.

"Yes," she breathed. "Ever since that night . . . oh, Stephen, just like that . . ."

He swiveled his thumb around her clit, and she moaned, her pussy milking his cock with renewed strength. He lifted her, pumping a little more intently into her. She pressed her body against his, her breasts crushed against his chest as she dug her fingernails into his back. He cupped her buttock with his other hand as he kept thrusting, his back tense as a bowstring, his legs tight with the exertion.

She was breathing in fast, hard gasps, her thighs clenched around him tightly. "Oh my God," she whispered. "Oh, Stephen . . . please . . . please . . ."

He paused. "Are you all right?"

"Don't stop!" She twisted her hips, coiled in the throes of sexual torment.

Her pussy clutched at him, and he groaned loudly. He thrust into her, high and hard, and she cried out. He felt her rippling release, and it goaded his own. He poured himself into her . . . or rather, into the condom, inside of her. He leaned forward, pinning her against the wall, the cool tiles a marked contrast from the warm water. His breathing was labored.

After long moments, he pulled away. Her expression was hard.

"Get off of me," she said quietly.

He realized, despite what had just happened, that nothing materially had changed, and he let her go, steeling himself for the real battle ahead.

Beth's emotions were at war. She knew she shouldn't have given in, but when she felt his hot, naked flesh against hers . . . when she'd felt the broad, blunt head of his cock pressing against her sensitive ache, her body had hijacked her common sense. And when he'd penetrated her, she genuinely didn't care what he'd done or what he might do in the future. All she knew was, in that moment, the man she'd been dying to have inside her for the past three days was finally where he belonged, playing her body like a virtuoso, and the tension that had been pushing her to the breaking point was finally finding a release. When she climaxed, it was as if every wish she'd ever made came true in one instant, in a crescendo of glorious rapture.

Then sanity returned.

"What are you going to do?" she asked.

He stood back, naked, his body looking sinewy and slick and still more compelling than anything she'd ever seen in her life. She crossed her arms in front of her bare breasts, feeling more vulnerable than sheer nudity could account for.

"Maybe we ought to get dressed," he suggested.

She dried off, handing him the damp towel afterward and then hastily putting on her day clothes. He did the same, his clothes clinging to his still moist skin. She fought not to stare at the way the cloth molded to his muscular form.

"First of all, I swear to God I had no idea who you were when I . . . when we . . ." He stammered, obviously struggling with his words. "When we got together," he finally stated.

Got together. How . . . limiting.

"And now that you know?" she prompted, tucking her hair into her veil.

He grimaced. "I don't want to hurt you," he said, and his voice was raw. "I report things, but my stories are meant to help, not hurt. I expose bad guys, make sure they can't keep doing what they're doing." He stared at her. "You've done nothing wrong."

She felt her muscles slowly lose their granitelike tension, and she almost collapsed to the floor, the relief was so sharp and sudden. "Thank you," she breathed, her heart in her words.

"But I have to know," he said. "Why here? Why for so long?"

She sighed. "I . . . was in trouble," she said. *To put it mildly.*

He nodded. "The Queen, right? Your stepmother."

The mere mention of the woman was enough to cause a wave of nervous nausea to creep over her. Beth clamped down on the emotion. "She wanted me dead."

Stephen's eyes widened. "Do you have proof of this?"

Beth shook her head. "Nothing I could use. There were those in the palace who knew what she was going to do," she said. "One of them helped me fake my death, after I paid him everything I had hidden away. But otherwise, everyone in the palace is loyal to her. They have to be." She shivered, remembering what had happened to the few servants who had tried to defend her.

Stephen put a hand on her shoulder. She started to shrug it away, but his palm was warm and comforting and she decided to enjoy the sensation, if only for a moment. She couldn't remember the last time she'd felt comforted in a physical sense.

She frowned. It'd been some time since she'd felt comforted in any way by another person, male or female.

"I made it to the U.S. with a fake passport," she said. "But I didn't have enough money, and the Queen was still looking for me. Everywhere I turned, I could see my own face in a newspaper, on a magazine rack. Then I found the Penitents . . . or rather, the Founders discovered me. They took me in, asked no questions. I've been safe here."

"You've been hidden here," he corrected. "It's been ten years. Haven't you thought about . . . maybe leaving?"

Now she pulled away from him. "Why would I?"

"Because there's more to life than hand washing clothes in a river, avoiding television, and staying separate from men until you die."

"It's not that bad," she hedged. "For the most part, I've enjoyed living here. I don't mind the work: I enjoy the nature, and the beauty, and the . . . the simplicity of it all."

He looked stubborn. "Yet you still slept with me."

"Yes." She cleared her throat. "And I don't regret it. I'd do it again." In fact, she wanted to do it again. She'd just had sex, but her body craved the sensations like a drug.

"What would you do if I weren't here anymore?"

The mere thought sent a wave of anxiety through her. "You're leaving?"

"I said, I'm a reporter," he replied. "I never meant to stay here. I was just supposed to pretend to be one of them, find out the story behind these crazy people, and then sneak right back out. This isn't the place for me." He paused, then his green eyes turned entreating. "This isn't the place for you either. *Bianca*."

She winced. She hadn't heard her real name in years. It sounded alien . . . and threatening.

"I'm Goodmaid Beth now," she answered.

"You can't keep hiding who you are."

"Watch me."

He let out an exasperated snort. "I can't believe you'd just . . . *settle* for this."

Funny, how she hadn't thought of it as "settling" until recently. Up until she'd found the Compound, fear and survival seemed to be all she knew. It justified her existence. "Have you ever had anyone try to kill you?"

To her surprise, he paused, looking up for a second. "When you say try to kill, do you mean premeditated, or sort of heat-of-the-moment?" He laughed. "Either way, yeah, a few."

It nonplussed her. "Who's tried to kill you?" Beth asked.

"Remember those bad people I write about?" His smile was quicksilver and devilish. "They generally don't like being stopped. Sometimes they try to get some payback on an exposé. Others just figure out I'm a reporter a little too early, and try some extreme methods to shut me up."

She stared at him, aghast. "And you're wondering why *I'm* doing what I'm doing? What are you, insane?"

"I don't let it stop me," he said, and his voice was serious. "Because I know what I'm doing is important. Besides . . . it's who I am."

"Yeah, well, try living your entire life with paparazzi hassling you and a crazed bitch plotting to kill you at any opportunity," she muttered. "Then judge me for living here."

They stood, silent, squaring off for a moment. Then he shook his head, taking a physical and metaphorical step back.

"I didn't come here to fight with you," he said. "Like I said, I don't want to hurt you. I just . . . I couldn't leave with this between us."

That pang again. "When are you leaving?"

"I don't know," he said. "Soon. Probably."

Some part of her wanted to beg him to stay. She clamped down on the impulse.

"But I had to see you." His voice sounded puzzled. Troubled.

"I'm glad you did." There were sounds of women, coming

closer. "You have to go," she said, fear creeping into her voice.

"I know."

Without warning, he leaned forward, kissing her hard. She kissed him back without thought or reservation.

"I'll come to your window tonight," he said.

She simply nodded. For all she knew, tonight might be all she had with him.

She wanted to make it memorable.

Beth deliberately shirked her afternoon of clothes washing, dragging her feet while cleaning the kitchen. It was a delivery day, she knew . . . and Lydia was waiting to process the order.

While she wouldn't necessarily consider Lydia a friend, Beth had to admire the way the woman made a priority of feeding her sexual appetites—and doing so with both enthusiasm and skill. She might put up a good front to please the Founders and keep her secret life hidden, but when she was in the moment, she was insatiable. Beth felt sure that Lydia could probably make a man like Stephen go crazy with desire, then she'd make him feel like a king as she brought him to release . . . all the while getting her own pleasure.

Beth wanted to do that: she wanted to bring Stephen— and herself as well—the most pleasure possible. But if he was leaving, she didn't have any time for a slow, trial-and-error education. She needed the advice of an expert.

Lydia smirked when she saw her. "Did you want something?" The words seemed to have a double meaning.

Beth cleared her throat. "Is the delivery woman coming today?"

Lydia's smirk widened into a smug grin. "More condoms already?" she drawled. "My, my. You *have* been busy."

Lydia had no idea. For a change, Beth didn't blush. "I could use some more," she admitted, with a strange sort of pride.

"Still not going to tell me who, *hmm?* Well . . . maybe I can guess." Lydia tapped a finger on her lips, pretending to mull it over. "Perhaps it's that burly Goodman Joshua? He seems to like you quite a bit. Or Goodman Victor. He's older, but he's got big hands."

Beth choked.

"Of course, it could be one of the newcomers. That Goodman Stephen, maybe . . ." Lydia's eyes glowed. "I'll bet he's huge."

Beth had no idea how to respond to that, so she kept silent.

"He carries himself well, too. If you hadn't gotten to him, I might've." Lydia's grin turned wicked. "I still may."

Beth didn't realize how angered she was until she was only inches from Lydia's grinning face, her hands bunched in fists. She didn't respond

Lydia looked amused and unafraid, but she still took a step back. "So secretive. That's cute."

Beth now reconsidered asking the woman for advice in anything, much less sex.

"But you need to consider: men are fickle, and whoever he is, he's going to be here a long, long time," Lydia said, and Beth felt a renewed sense of unease. *No, he's not.* "You both are. You can be territorial, but it's not like you two can be married or have anything else lasting without keeping it a secret. Even if you could, would he want that?" Lydia shrugged. "Probably not. Which means you'll be watching him walk away at some point—maybe moving to another affair. Why let yourself get hurt? Why not simply enjoy what you have now, then enjoy something else, with *someone else*, later?"

She sounded so imminently practical. So unemotional. It was as if she were a purely physical creature.

She reminded Beth of her stepmother in a certain way. The thought wasn't comforting.

"Delivery," a croaking voice called out. Beth turned. The delivery woman shuffled in, her eyes bird-bright and inquisitive. "Sorry. Didn't mean to interrupt such an interesting conversation."

Beth squirmed uncomfortably. Lydia simply shrugged.

"Did you get what I ordered?"

The woman's eyes narrowed at Lydia's peremptory tone. "Of course I did," she said sharply. "That's my *job*, isn't it?"

Lydia didn't notice the scorn or irritation, it seemed. When she wasn't under the watchful eye of the Penitents or one of the Founders, Beth noticed that Lydia was as single-minded as a rich only child on her birthday. "Where is it?"

"Hold your horses," the delivery woman said, reaching into a box. She glanced around, then pulled out a black corset, with a red rose between the cups of the brassiere top. Lydia grinned, holding it up to her chest furtively.

"This will make them go wild," Lydia said, plumping up her breasts as best she could in her shapeless gray shift, as if imagining the results of the new garment.

The delivery woman nodded. "Corsets are popular. Although a lot can be said for a simple bra and thong combination, worn properly."

Lydia looked at the woman in revulsion. "I think I know about seduction, thanks very much."

For a second, there was a look of bare fury on the delivery woman's face, but then it shifted back to its normal state. Beth wondered if she'd really witnessed it, or if it were simply the odd configuration of the woman's features, since the expression seemed to melt away in a blink. Perhaps she'd imagined it.

The woman seemed to notice Beth's scrutiny, because she turned her large, protruding eye toward her. "And you, dearie? Did you reconsider my offer? What can I tempt you with today?"

Lydia laughed, tucking the corset in a burlap bag. "She just needs more condoms," she said.

"Really." The delivery woman looked at her speculatively. "You don't say."

Beth blushed, glaring at Lydia. "And . . ." She stumbled on the words.

"And?"

"If you've got any . . . other lingerie . . . or something," Beth stammered.

"Oho!" The delivery woman laughed. "I see. Trying to drive *your* somebody wild, eh?"

Lydia rolled her eyes. Beth ignored her.

"I won't now, but perhaps next time. You'd be, what, a size four?" She glanced over Beth's frame, then, to her shock, ran her hands over her sides. "Four. I'll get you something in a few weeks, don't worry."

"I may not have until next time," Beth said hastily. Lydia's eyebrows jumped up toward her scalp, but Beth plowed onward. "What do you have readily available?"

"I'm not a portable department store," the delivery woman said, "but I can see what I've got . . ." She disappeared, back toward her truck.

"What do you mean, you might not have until next time?" Lydia asked.

"It's not your business."

"Are you losing his interest that quickly, then?"

Beth finally lost her temper. "He might not be here."

Lydia's eyes widened in surprise. "Nobody ever *leaves* here. It's one of the reasons my parents put me here."

"Yes, well, there's always a first time," Beth muttered.

"Did he ask you to go with him?" Lydia whispered.

Beth sighed, then nodded.

"And . . . you won't go?"

Beth nodded again.

"Would he stay?"

Beth closed her eyes for a second. "No," she finally answered, the word tearing at her throat. "I don't think so."

Lydia's forehead furrowed. "You're letting him have too much power, then," she pronounced.

"What?" Beth scoffed. "Lydia, do you even know what you're talking about?"

"Trust me. I was having sex with a boy from the high school, on the outside," Lydia said, "and I thought I loved him. He threw me away, started dating some other girl. I made him want me again. Teased him. Made love with him even while he was still seeing her. Made him crazy with it.

Finally took him back . . ." She smiled. "Then I threw *him* away."

"How?" Beth asked, reluctantly fascinated.

"You've just got to know what men want," Lydia said breezily. "They want a woman who's innocent, but still willing to do anything. They like confidence and love feeling wanted. They want a woman who's brave enough to do anything, absolutely anything, to feel pleasure." Lydia closed her eyes, rubbing her hand unconsciously against her stomach. "They like a woman who likes sex and isn't afraid to show it."

Before Beth could ask more questions, the delivery woman returned. "This is all I've got on short notice," she said, handing a small, tissue-wrapped package over. "It's not your size, but I don't think it'll be that much bigger. I meant it for this one," gesturing to Lydia, "but she told me she's got very specific tastes."

It was a dark blue teddy, sheer lace, a very simple pattern. All that covered the back was a few thin straps . . . including up the backside, which was a thong.

Beth blushed.

"It's never been worn," the delivery woman assured her. "I was going to return it."

"It's too plain for me," Lydia said critically, "but I'll bet you could do something with it. Especially if he's not expecting it."

"Like what?"

Lydia smiled. "Just listen to me, very carefully. First, what you do . . ."

Chapter Eight

I've got to get her out of here.

It was purely selfish, Stephen knew. First of all, if he could get her to agree to leave the Compound with him, he'd help her get her life back . . . and he'd have the exclusive on her story. From a career standpoint, that alone would be enormous. But even if it took some persuading—even if she just agreed to leave the Compound and hide somewhere else for a while—he'd have *her*.

That, he had to admit, had an even greater appeal, from a completely personal standpoint, albeit an equally selfish one.

The problem was she had everything she wanted here. She loved the lifestyle. She liked the work. The only thing she'd conceded that the life was missing was sex.

He was determined to show her just how much she'd miss that when he was gone . . . and he wanted to help her realize that she couldn't get what she had with him with just anyone. Whether he liked it or not, the two of them were linked somehow, and he wasn't about to let her go without a struggle, even if it were a sexual one.

He felt sure that they'd both enjoy it, no matter who won. He smiled slowly as he got closer to her window, his body going hard in a rush.

Let the battles begin.

The window was open, as were the shutters: a good sign. He climbed into the darkened room, then struggled to make her out. He turned, closing the window and shutter behind him, plunging him into complete pitch-black. "Beth? Where are you?"

He expected her to turn on the light. Instead, he felt her hands on him, like a succubus, mysterious and compelling. She unbuttoned his shirt, slipping it off his shoulders, then stroked down his sides and legs. He felt his shoes loosen, and he responded by kicking them off. She peeled off his socks, then undid his pants, slowly unzipping the fly. He took a deep breath, inhaling her unique floral scent. He reached out blindly, bumping against soft skin and silken hair.

"I want to see you," he said.

Her laugh was ghostly, disembodied. "Not yet. I want to remember what you feel like in the darkness."

So she had already accepted him leaving, and was prepared to let him go. His jaw clenched. He had his work cut out for him.

Her fingertips breezed over him, caressing each line of his arms, his neck, his chest. She tugged down his pants and boxers slowly, letting them pool around his ankles. He kicked them away, standing naked and erect.

When her fingertips brushed against his cock, he took in a hissing breath.

He felt her breath warm the skin of his cock head, and he leaned forward, brushing it against her lips. She laughed again softly, cupping his balls for an instant. Then she raked her short, round nails down his thighs. He groaned as the sensation rang through his genitals like a bell, radiating outward.

The touch dissipated, replaced by soft, wet kisses on his abdomen. His stomach muscles tightened instinctively, and he put his hand out, stroking the downy softness of her hair. He felt the flick of her tongue across his navel, trailing a moist line up his chest. Her fingertips danced over his hips, and he sighed.

He'd never been with a woman like this before . . . dark, exciting, and wholly unexpected. He also wasn't used to being at the mercy of a woman exploring him in the dark.

She touched him everywhere she could reach. She kneaded his shoulders, then his lower back. She stroked the area between his ass and his balls, tickling it experimentally. He growled in appreciation. She made little sounds of her own, in obvious admiration of his arms, his hands. She sucked on his fingertips.

She was making him crazy.

He turned, guessing where she was, reaching for her. Her long hair brushed over his hands, but she was too quick, too used to the darkness and the room. He took a step forward, feeling the quilt under his feet, then his shin hit the metal bed frame. "Goddammit," he said, barely stopping himself from falling over. "This isn't fair."

"Sorry," she said, sounding contrite. "It'd be easier if you just stood still and let me touch you."

"Sweetheart, you don't know me very well if you think I'd be satisfied with just being touched," he replied, trying to keep his tone light. But her thorough investigation of his body in the darkness had only stoked the flames of desire inside him, and now it was raging out of control.

"That's the thing. I don't know you," she said. "I'm trying to get to know you."

"I want to touch you," he said. "I *need* to touch you."

He heard the naked longing in his voice, and it disturbed him. He'd never begged for a woman in his life. Why the fuck was he doing it now?

"I'm going to turn on the light," she said, and he heard her padding footsteps as she went over to the table. As his eyes adjusted, he took in what she was wearing. His mouth went dry, and his body went still as stone.

She was wearing a one-piece teddy, in a shimmering, translucent purple-blue that reminded him of her eyes. The legs were cut high on her thighs, and her nipples were suggestive shadows beneath the sheer material, as was the curly black hair covering her pussy. Her hair was pulled up in a loose knot, with waves tumbling to frame her face. She looked like a cross between a fairy tale princess and a wet dream, and he wanted her.

"Do . . . do you like it?"

He couldn't believe the hesitation in her voice. He swallowed hard. "Where did you get it?"

She shrugged. "Same place I got the condoms," she said, and she tugged at the top of the material, shifting it over her cleavage. "I wasn't sure what I looked like—they don't allow mirrors, and it wasn't like I could wear this to the stream. I don't look like an idiot?"

She really *was* unsure of her appearance. Her pale skin was flushed with excitement: her cheeks were tinted a delicate pink, and her blue eyes sparkled. She looked amazing.

He knew that he couldn't answer her and do it justice. Instead, he did what he'd been begging for.

He touched her.

He stroked the material, tracing the edges of the fabric, first with his fingertip, then with his tongue. He sucked at her left nipple through the sheer teddy, soaking through it to get to her. She gasped, her head tilting back, causing more waves of hair to tumble around her face. She gripped the back of his neck and one of his shoulders as he increased the pressure, drawing more of her into his mouth, laving the breast ravenously. He reached down, pushing aside the small swath of fabric between her thighs. She was already wet, dripping for him. "God, Beth," he whispered against her skin. "You're amazing. And you look phenomenal." He pulled back, looking in her eyes to emphasize his point. "I didn't think I could want you more than I have, but . . . I want to be inside you. I want to slide my cock inside your wet, warm pussy, and I want to stroke your clit with every single thrust. I want you to feel me, sweetheart. I want you to call my name when you come."

She shivered, biting her lip as she rubbed her thighs together, against his fingertip. He plunged it in deeper, and she gasped.

"W-wait," she said.

His hand paused. "Wait?"

"Remember when you said, that first night, that if I kept touching you, you'd lose control?"

He smiled. "It's okay if you lose control," he said, moving his finger slightly, loving the way her body shivered against him.

"But . . . I want to make you feel . . . like you make me feel. I want to show you."

He smiled. She said it with such sweet frustration.

"Later," he said, holding her close to him, moving his hand slowly and lovingly against her sopping wet pussy. "Right now, just enjoy it . . ."

She cried out softly, her head resting against his shoulder, her hair stroking across his bare skin in ticklish-soft waves. Her nipples were erect, dragging across his chest as his hand kept moving. She reached down between them, grasping his cock in her fingertips, stroking against the head as he continued his relentless onslaught. He closed his eyes, focusing for a second on the feel of those fingers, wrapping around the hard length of him, stroking in featherlight, maddening touches.

Then she released him, clutching at his shoulders, opening her legs wider. Her breathing went shallow and quick, and she rocked her hips against his hand. He felt her body clench around his fingers, and he suckled on her breast again.

"*Stephen!*" She threw her head back, slamming her pussy against his hand as he plunged deeper into her, searching for and finding her G-spot and prolonging the release. His cock was already weeping pre-come It was all he could do not to plunge inside of her, feel the glorious aftershocks of her orgasm clenching around his shaft.

But tonight wasn't about him, it was about her.

He smiled as she collapsed against him. He was looking forward to showing her what else he could do . . . and that there were even more delights they could share, if only she'd leave the Compound with him.

Beth struggled to regain her composure. As her orgasm-fogged mind cleared, she remembered Lydia's words of advice.

If you can't control yourself, you can't seduce him. It's that simple.

She moved away from him, trying to catch her breath. He was smiling, affectionate, but at the same time, a little smug.

"How was that?" he asked.

"Incredible," she said truthfully. "But it always is with you. You know that."

"I'm not sure," he teased. "We'll need to try it again to make sure . . ."

"No, now it's your turn," she said. "There are some things I want to try."

He looked puzzled by her intensity, but he shrugged. "I'll be happy to help out."

Now she smiled. "Why don't you get on the bed?"

"This bed?" He pointed to her narrow cot. "Uh . . . okay. But are you sure we'll be comfortable? I thought you said we both wouldn't fit on it."

"For this, we will," she said, her mind desperately replaying Lydia's detailed advice. "Just lie down."

He did as he was told, for which she was grateful. She was nervous enough—although she had to admit, that pounding orgasm did take a great deal of the edge off. She let out a tiny laugh at the thought.

One of Stephen's eyebrows went up. "Something funny?"

She looked over his naked body, taking up most of her bed. He looked like he was carved out of marble, but she knew firsthand how marvelously hot-blooded his flesh was. She stroked her hands over the length of him. "No," she breathed. "Not funny at all." Then she looked in his eyes. "You make me very happy."

His green eyes were dark with passion. "I'm glad."

She hadn't meant to say that. Lydia would say that she was giving away her power. But it was the truth: he *did* make her happy, happier than she'd been in more years than she could remember. So even if tonight failed, and he still walked away, she would at least have tonight.

She took his cock into her mouth.

He gasped, obviously unready for her direct approach. "Sweet Jesus," he groaned, as she took a long, drawing pull, slowly letting him withdraw from her. Not too hard . . . a blowjob was not a suck job, she remembered. She took him back into her mouth, wrapping her tongue around the underside of his cock head, tasting the salty drop of moisture from the tip. She explored the narrow fissure with her tongue, then grazed it with her teeth. She was gratified when he shivered, and she looked up to find his eyes closed, his hands clenched around the bars of her headboard.

She made sure his cock was nice and moist, then she stroked the length of him with firm, determined grips of her right hand. With her left, she cupped his balls gently . . . then she licked her finger, and rubbed against the flat patch of skin just behind his balls, before the cleft of his buttocks. He moaned, his hips raising off the bed. "Do you like that?" she asked curiously.

"How . . . how the hell . . ."

She took that as a yes. She took him in her mouth again for one long, loving taste. Then she reached for the condom she'd tucked by the side of the wall, opening the packet.

Carefully, remembering Lydia's advice, she rolled the condom on him with her mouth. His hips rose to meet her, and she took him as deep as possible, rolling it the rest of the way with her fingers. When she looked up to see him, staring at her in wonder, she didn't even mind the taste of the latex.

"Did you read a book or something?"

"I decided I wanted to try a few new things," she replied. "Is it working?"

"Depends. What did you have in—"

Before he could finish the sentence, she turned, presenting him with the crossed-strap back of her lingerie. She heard his deep, harsh inhalation of breath. "Very nice," he said, his voice sounding strained.

She straddled him, but facing away from him, moving the thin material of the thong out of the way of his probing cock. She hoped that this would work as well as Lydia had said it would, and lowered herself onto him.

"*Mmmmm,*" he said, as she closed around him. "Nice view."

It felt different, letting him enter her this way. She rose slightly, then pressed onto him again, feeling his cock penetrate her by inches. He reached forward, gripping her buttocks, and she felt a little thrill as she swiveled her hips. She kept moving, slowly, carefully.

Suddenly, she felt his muscles ripple beneath her, and she realized he was sitting up. "May I?" he whispered in her ear.

"Did I do it wrong?" she asked, nervous.

"Not at all." She could hear desire, thick in his voice. "I just thought we might try . . ."

He cupped one hand over her breast, the other between her legs, his cock trapped inside her. She gasped at the sensation washing over her. He sucked on her neck, hard enough to mark her, and the slight pain felt heavenly, making her almost wild with need.

She bucked against him, and he held on tight, shifting her against his cock.

"More," she said, her own voice harsh. "You make me so wet, Stephen. I love the feel of your cock inside me . . ."

"Baby," he whispered against her shoulder, then with a fluid motion, he turned her to face him, plunging inside her. She threw herself against him, flexing her hips and slamming against his hardness, clawing at his back. "God, your pussy is so tight . . ."

"Fuck me," she said, wrapping her legs around his waist, tugging at the hair at the nape of his neck. "Fuck me *hard*."

If she shocked him, she was past the point of caring. He rolled her over, thrusting harder into her, and she tilted her pelvis. Then he grasped one leg, resting it over his shoulder . . . then the other. He was so deep inside her, she thought he might touch her heart. He slid into her all the way up to his balls, the whole hard length of him surrounded by her willing flesh, and she cried out.

"Am I hurting you?" he asked, through gritted teeth.

"Deeper!" she ordered, her head lolling back and forth, and she rolled her nipples between her fingertips, relishing the unbelievable sensation that triangulated between her breasts and her pussy. The beginning tremors of orgasm were signaling, and she didn't fight it. "I'm going to come, Stephen, don't stop, don't ever stop . . ."

He seemed to snap. He pounded against her like a rampaging animal, battering her with his cock, and she squeezed her buttocks tight, keeping her pussy clenched around him like a fist as the orgasm shot through her in a drowning wave. She cried out his name, and he groaned and kept pounding against her, his flesh shuddering. Her orgasm stretched out like taffy, coming back again and again, submerging her in slow, repeating bursts each time he slammed his cock full hilt inside her.

He collapsed on top of her, his full weight crushing her. She gasped, and he rolled them both on to her bare floor. Their faces were framed by the veil of her hair.

"That . . . was fucking . . . incredible," he said, when he could finally speak.

She smiled, kissing him. He kissed her back, and it was hot and wet and just like their lovemaking—ravenous.

"We're just getting started," she said. "There are a few more things I want to try."

"Sweetheart, I've got to go," Stephen said, after a few hours had passed. "It's starting to get light."

She nuzzled against him, and he marveled once again at finding her. Especially the way she'd been tonight.

There was nothing, it seemed, that she wasn't willing to try, if she thought it would bring him pleasure. She was like a nymphomaniac. And his cock, bless it, surprised him by continually rising to the challenge. They'd fucked three times . . . the first time on the bed, then once against the windowsill, then once on the floor.

When they got on the outside, they'd have to look into getting her on the birth control pill. The thought of getting inside her welcoming wetness fully naked, without the barrier of a rubber between them, was almost enough to get him hard again. It was as if someone had slipped him Viagra or something. He'd never gotten it up this many times, in this short a period, before.

It was because of her, and he knew it.

"I don't want you to leave," she said, cuddled against his chest on the quilt they'd spread on the floor.

"I don't want to leave, either," he said, and he meant it. "But if they find me in the women's dormitory, I think we'd both be in trouble, don't you?"

"I know," she said. To his surprise, he felt hot wetness against his chest, and he nudged her up so he could look at her face.

She had tears in her eyes. It stabbed at his heart. "What's wrong?" he asked, smoothing a wayward teardrop as it streaked down her cheek.

"I may never see you again," she whispered.

He swallowed hard. This was it. The make or break moment. "It doesn't have to be like that," he said.

She got up, stepping away from him, and he propped himself up on one elbow. "I wasn't going to say anything," she said, hugging herself as if cold. "I just wanted to have one incredible night with you, and then I thought I could let you go. So at least I'd have memories."

Suddenly, it all made sense. He knew she enjoyed sex with him, but tonight it was as if she'd unleashed a nymphomaniac . . . she was making love as if it were her last chance on earth. And now, he realized, that's exactly what it was. For her.

He got up, enfolding her in his arms. "You could leave here."

She went still in his arms, and he turned to study her expression. She was still crying, her violet eyes looking luminous.

"I'd be found," she said softly. "I'd be *killed*. Don't you understand that?"

"I'd protect you," he promised.

"But I'm safe here," she said.

"Don't you want to be with me?"

She stared at him. "Couldn't I ask you the same question?"

"Of course I want to be with you. But it's different," he said, shoving away any guilt that might be plaguing him. "If you left with me, you'd be . . . accepting who you are. Getting out of this—this *cult*."

"Accepting who I am," she said, with a small, bitter laugh. "Which means making me a target."

He bit back a curse. "I swear, I'd die before I let anybody hurt you."

She looked surprised at that one, which mirrored what he

felt at the same sentence. But, having said it, he realized he meant it.

"Come with me," he whispered. "I promise I'll keep you safe."

"You can't promise that." She didn't sound sad, or wistful, or whining. She sounded practical. Resigned.

He sighed. He hadn't convinced her. But she was wearing down. He knew it.

"When are you leaving?" she asked, her voice sounding like a strained effort at being casual.

He ought to leave soon, just a few days. But now, with this, with her . . . he needed to think about it. He needed more time.

"I don't know," he said honestly.

She turned in his arms, facing him. "I thought you had to leave right away."

"Nothing's set in stone," he said. "I could stay a little while longer."

She smiled, and he got hit with it again—that heroic feeling. A fellow could get addicted to that feeling, if he weren't already hooked to everything else Beth had to offer.

"If you stay," she said, and there was a teasing little grin on her face, "I'll make it worth your while."

He smiled back, but even as he let the mood lighten, he realized that, on some level, he was actually considering it.

He shook his head.

"If I stay too long, you're gonna kill me with sex, woman," he said with a wink.

But what a way to go . . .

* * *

"Where are you going, Goodman Stephen?" Founder Timothy asked.

"Bathroom break, Founder," Stephen lied, trying to make his voice sound as docile as possible. Which, admittedly, wasn't easy for him.

"Well, don't take all day." Founder Timothy turned back to oversee the other Penitents, working in the mine.

Stephen ducked out of the shaft, heading for the office building. He walked past the restrooms and instead went straight for the pay phone, dialing his editor in New York.

"Calling me collect?" His editor, Randall, sounded amused. "Tell me you've got the story in the bag. I've got another assignment I need you on, ASAP."

Stephen winced. "Actually, that's why I'm calling. This assignment's going to take a little longer than we thought."

"Are you kidding?" Randall's voice went up an octave, a bad sign. "Jesus Christ, Stephen, I sent you off to go undercover with those butter churners to teach you a lesson, not because I expected you to dig up any dirt. It's a puff piece, not an Enron scandal! What's the holdup?"

"The story's not finished. All my facts are still questionable, and the lawyers would have a field day," Stephen protested, his excuse sounding lame to his own ears. "Besides, I'm following more leads, getting a few more interviews. They've got a whole banishment thing that sounds, er, promising."

"Bullshit." Stephen could practically hear the vein throbbing in Randall's temple. "Okay, I shouldn't have sent you on a wild goose chase to punish you for maxing out your expense card. Mea culpa, all right? But I need you, like *yesterday*, on a real story. Serious undercover—high-tech forgery at a lead-

ing computer company. You can't tell me that doesn't get you
hot and bothered, either. It's right up your alley. So unless
you think you're bucking for a Pulitzer with these throwback
farm folk, get your ass back to the office by no later than tomorrow. Clear?"

High-tech forgery. Stephen had an interest in computers,
and with a big company involved in forgery—Randall was
right, it was the sort of story that made his mouth water. And
any other time, he'd leap at it, no matter what other story he
was working on. "I'm telling you, Randall, I can't just cut
and run."

There was a pause on the other end of the line. "You're not
just being pissy, then," Randall said slowly. "You're actually
turning down a dream assignment so you can stay with these
Amish knockoffs."

"I wouldn't put it that way, but yeah."

"Jesus." Randall let out a low whistle. "You're not burning
out on me, are you?"

"No," Stephen said, offended. "Of course not."

"It's not so far-fetched. You've been berserk for work for,
what, five years now? Ever since I hired you, I've never known
you to have anything but the mildest of social lives . . . and
even then, I think it was largely to keep networks open for
your stories." Randall sighed. "You're a hell of a reporter, but
how you've pushed it this close to the edge without slipping
off has been something of a miracle."

"Oh, come off it," Stephen scoffed. "Everybody works this
hard at the office, Rand. You know that."

"Actually, there's a running bet with the other reporters

on how you're going to melt down," Randall said, surprising Stephen. "Even money, split between you turning into a paper-pants-wearing occupant of some ashram in India, and you becoming some kind of foreign legionnaire in a desert somewhere."

"Ha-fucking-ha, boss," Stephen said impatiently. "Listen, I—"

"Me, I had twenty toward you going up in a clock tower with a high-powered rifle," Randall said mildly. "Guess you shocked us all by going rural. . . ."

"Will you listen to me!" Stephen snapped. "I'm sitting on maybe the biggest story of both our lives here. I can't say what it is, and you wouldn't believe me if I told you anyway, but *trust me*. This one's huge."

Randall was quiet. The silence was filled with a tangible doubt.

"You know me," Stephen said. "No bullshit. I just need more time."

Randall sighed. "Okay. One week." Before Stephen could argue, Randall cut him off. "After that, I don't care if they're cloning Paris Hilton or you've found weapons of mass destruction hidden in their goddamn granaries, you're back here or you're fired. Got it?"

Stephen clenched his jaw. "All right. One week." He hung up the phone, then headed back, hoping he wasn't missed.

Founder Timothy was waiting for him at the mine entrance, arms crossed, expression stern. It would've been more imposing if Founder Timothy hadn't been quite so short, plump, and balding. "You certainly took your time,

Goodman Stephen," he said sourly. "I was just coming to fetch you."

"Intestinal issues," Stephen said glibly. He started to head back to the job, but Timothy stepped in front of him, blocking his way.

"The Penitent tenets of belief command humility," Timothy said, his tone of a high school teacher . . . one that all the students loathed getting. "You'd do well to learn some humility, Goodman Stephen. Otherwise, we might be forced to school some into you."

Stephen stared at Founder Timothy in disbelief. Did the man actually think he was being menacing? It was like getting bullied by a Teletubby, for pity's sake. Stephen fought hard not to laugh.

"Believe me, boy," Timothy said, and there was a sadistic gleam in his watery gray eyes, "you don't want the Founders taking an undue interest in your discipline."

Now Stephen shifted uneasily. Like Amos, this guy had a supersized portion of crazy tucked behind his harmless-farmer exterior. There was more going on in the Penitents than met the eye, clearly. They probably wouldn't make a bad story, at that.

But he didn't care right now, couldn't delve into it. All that mattered was Beth.

"I'm sorry, Founder," Stephen muttered contritely, looking at the ground.

"All right, then," Timothy said, sounding slightly mollified. "You have my permission to go back to work."

Stephen stalked back into the mine, annoyed by the little

power play. His mind quickly raced past the incident to the matter at hand. One week. He had one week to convince Beth to leave the Penitent Compound behind. He prided himself on his skills of persuasion . . . after all, it was one of the things that made him a good reporter. But what, exactly, was he offering her?

I'd get killed. Her voice echoed in his soul.

If she left the Compound, at best, she'd be plunged head-first into the fishbowl lifestyle of the missing Princess; at worst, she'd be the target of a score of professional hits from her vindictive stepmother, who was looking to protect her claim on the throne.

Stephen might be a pretty good lay, but she was right: no sex was worth what he was asking her to do. The thought of her dying, especially because *he asked her to*, was more than he could bear.

So where did that leave him?

Where did that leave *them*?

He ought to let her go—that was the noble thing to do, probably the right thing to do. After all, she was happy in the Compound. Well, if not happy, at least she was content, and most important, she was safe. He should just leave the place, tell Randall he'd had a mental aberration, and go on the next assignment. Maybe even schedule a vacation after that. He should do whatever he had to, to forget he'd ever seen Beth, aka the Princess.

Or touched her.

Or tasted her . . .

He grimaced.

Like hell.

His whole body rebelled at the thought of being apart from her. He slammed his pickax into a sheet of rock, the force reverberating up his arms, all the way to his spine. A shower of stone fragments flew at him like shrapnel.

"Watch it!" Timothy barked, as others ducked out of the way, grumbling. "This isn't that difficult. Be careful!"

Stephen pulled the pick away, his arms sore. He forced himself to concentrate on the task at hand, but his mind kept wandering back to her.

He didn't want to leave her, couldn't stand the idea of being apart from her. What did that mean? Should he abandon his career, join the crazy-ass Penitents, and spend the rest of his life making love to Beth in secret . . . for as long as they didn't get caught?

His mind rebelled at that notion. His career was his life. And he knew, instinctively, that living with the Penitents was not something his independent streak would tolerate for any length of time.

His heart, strangely, had a sense of quiet resignation.

If that's what it takes . . .

He felt a sudden nausea, as if he were on a free-fall ride at a theme park. His pickax fell with a clatter.

He *was* falling, he realized. He was falling hard for Beth, a woman determined to stay hidden in this strange, secluded, cultlike world.

He had no choice. He had to do whatever he could to get her to leave—or else lose the one woman he'd finally fallen in love with.

Chapter Nine

Beth ushered Stephen into the empty kitchen of the Dining Hall, feeling like a traitor. Kitchens were domestic workplaces, strictly the Goodmaids' province. Stephen might be the first man in the area in the past fifteen years. Even the Founders avoided the place. But since the Founders avoided it, and since she knew that preparation for dinner wouldn't take place for hours, it was the safest place she could think of. Nonetheless, she silently led him to the pantry, so they had one more level of warning.

"What did you need to speak to me about so urgently?" she asked in a soft voice, still listening for any telltale footsteps of an intruder.

When she turned to look at him, he leaned in, kissing her roughly, and suddenly his arms were around her.

Just like that, all fear left her, flooded out by the rush of desire that always crashed over her when Stephen touched her.

"*Stephen,*" she breathed, and she threw herself into his arms, giving in full body to the kiss. The slide and press of his firm lips molding themselves to hers, his tongue searching the soft flesh inside her mouth, their tongues twining was enough to cause her to gasp in pleasure. She felt her breasts tighten and her pussy began to throb with need. Just like that, she marveled. All it took was a kiss, and her body already began to demand more.

What will I do when he leaves?

She forced the thought out of her head. "We shouldn't," she murmured, halfheartedly.

He sighed. "I know. But I couldn't help it." He didn't sound sorry, and his eyes glowed with passion.

Her hands itched to unbutton his fly, so she could see his rigid cock in daylight, rather than illuminated by a lamp. She knew he was hard—she'd felt the length of him press against her stomach as she'd pressed fully against his body. She felt the rush of wetness between her thighs, even more since she'd forgone underwear, and she could feel her natural lubrication seeping through her curls, making her thighs slick with each shifting brush between them.

Not that she'd planned this. But wandering through her daily chores, knowing at any moment that she *could* see Stephen, and possibly steal a moment . . .

She moaned softly as her body trembled.

"God, I want you," he breathed, nipping at her earlobe. She rubbed her pelvis against the front of his trousers, and he groaned. "But . . . we do need to talk."

"Right," she rasped. "Of course." She forced herself to take a step away from him, keeping her hands knotted behind her back.

He took a deep breath. "I spoke with my editor," Stephen said with a heavy voice, and Beth felt a chill cut through her ardor. "He says I have to be back in one week, or I'll be fired."

"One week?" Beth echoed faintly. The thought paralyzed her. She wasn't ready to let go of him. She didn't know if she'd ever be ready, but . . . "So, that's it, then? You're leaving in a week?"

He sighed. "I can't stay, Beth. You know that."

Disappointment curdled in her stomach. "Yes," she echoed softly. "I knew that."

He framed her face in his hands. "Which is why I'm asking you—no, I'm *begging* you—to come with me."

For a moment, she was hypnotized by the look of longing in his eyes. Then she pulled away. "You mean, leave this place?"

He nodded.

"I can't," she said.

"Why not? Honestly, what's keeping you here?" he asked, and his voice was insistent. "The hard labor? The hot, uncomfortable clothes? Or the fact that they treat women like second-class citizens?"

She pulled back, as if his words were a physical assault. "It's not . . ."

She started to say *it isn't that bad*, but her mind replayed a dozen scenes from her past, here at the Penitent Compound. Things that she'd cheerfully ignored. The fact that women did all the domestic chores had not initially bothered her—she'd just been grateful to have found a safe haven. But subconsciously, things *had* rankled.

Stephen nodded, staring into her eyes. "You know exactly what I'm talking about," he said.

She gritted her teeth. "I made the choice to come here," she said. "I knew what I was getting into."

"You knew what you were getting out of," he countered. "You made a decision when you were under duress. That was *ten years ago*. You were a child then." He held her, his hands spanning her hips, pulling her to him. "You're a woman now, Beth. You can make new choices."

The words were dizzying.

"I'll be killed," she whispered. "You don't understand. The Queen is relentless. She's got money. Power. She hates me. She'll do anything to see me dead. If she found out I'm alive . . ." Beth swallowed hard against the lump forming in her throat, choking on her childhood fears.

Stephen held her tight. "I will do anything on earth to protect you, Beth," he whispered fiercely. "I'd die if I had to."

She marveled at the sincerity in his tone, and held him tightly.

"I know it's selfish of me," he said, his voice ragged. "But I also know that this place isn't what you think it is. You don't need this place. I'll devote my life to keeping you safe. Whatever it takes."

As long as she could remember, she couldn't recall one time when someone had focused so purely on her needs and safety. Her own father, so wrapped up in the loss of her mother, had remarried and then ignored his daughter in an attempt to find some kind of anesthetic happiness with his new wife. Even the servant who had helped her escape from the palace had to be bribed richly for the service.

She did not see herself as a victim because of this. She was merely used to relying on herself. So Stephen's admission was staggering.

"You can't possibly mean it," she murmured, despite the little glow of hope warming her chest.

He kissed her, gently, tenderly. "Believe me, sweetheart. I've never been more serious in my life."

"But you don't even know me," she pressed on. *Why are you trying to ruin this? Why not just enjoy it?* "We've just . . . had sex." Abruptly, she remembered what Lydia had told her. "You'll get tired of it, and you'll want to move on." She bit her lip. "Won't you? Don't all men? God, I don't know about these things!"

"I'm not all men," he said. "And I've told you, this isn't just sex. You're different."

"I'm a princess," she agreed bitterly.

"No," he said. "You're Beth. You work hard and you don't complain, even though life has dealt you a pretty shitty hand. You're beautiful, but you see it as a curse to work around instead of a meal ticket, or a reason why the world owes you things. You've lived through tragedy and you're still able to enjoy just sitting out in a damned meadow, looking at some flowers. You're smart, and sweet, and even in a damned full-length harsh cotton dress and veil you're the hottest woman I've ever laid eyes on, and my cock gets hard if I smell a flower that reminds me of you. I don't know what it is, but I'm not going to fight it. I'm falling hard for you, Beth." He frowned. "You might not want to deal with it, but there it is."

She stared at him. Even here, no one seemed to understand her. They either saw her as "Goodmaid Beth," one of the Founders' favorites, but they projected what they wanted to see. He seemed to see her clearly, and he was falling in love with her.

She swallowed hard.

"I'm falling hard for you, too," she said softly.

He sighed. "I'm your first time. You don't know me."

"I know that you're used to being other people," she countered. "You pretend for your job, and your job is your life. So you're not even used to being yourself. I know you don't do well with authority . . ."

"Is it that obvious?" He laughed.

"But you'll put up with anything to finish what you set your mind to. You want to make things right, and punish people who are wrong. You protect people."

"Beth," he said, his expression pained, "I'm not as good a person as you think I am."

"Yes," she said, cupping the side of his face, "you are. You just can't see it."

"Maybe that's why I love you," he murmured. "Because of what you see in me."

She felt a thrill at hearing him say the words aloud. "And maybe I love you because you're willing to put everything in your life aside, just to protect me."

"Beth . . ."

He reached for her, and this time stopping him was the

last thing on her mind. She gave in to his embrace, melting into him like butter into toast.

"God, I want to touch you," he said. "Whenever I'm near you . . ."

"I know," she breathed. "I know. I need you."

They kissed in a frenzy, hands touching everywhere. Her veil slipped from her head, her braids tumbling out loosely. He stroked her hair, her face, down the curve of her neck to her chest. She ran her nails down his stomach, undoing the buttons of his trousers.

He inhaled sharply. "We'll get caught," he cautioned, even as his hips leaned toward her.

"I don't care," she said recklessly, but when he started to pull away, she tugged at him. "No one's supposed to be in here for a few hours. We can be quick." She kissed him hard, slipping his cock free of its restraints. It sprang to life, gloriously full, already a dark purple with need. "I want to feel you inside me . . ."

"*Beth*," he breathed, as she stroked the velvety smooth tip of his penis. He fumbled in his pocket for a condom, tearing the package open with his teeth. For a brief second, she resented the barrier, wondering what he would feel like, naked inside of her. But even that was too dangerous for them, and despite the desire pumping through her veins, she wasn't so far gone not to realize the dangers.

What if they had a child?

She hadn't thought about having children, or a family . . . not for years, since she was a child, before her mother died. Now, the thought brought up a wistful longing.

He slid the condom on, and she reached for him. He tugged

up her skirt, then reached between her legs. He made a growl of approval. "You're not wearing underwear."

She spread her legs, holding her skirt up. "I've been thinking of you all day," she answered. "I didn't know we'd get the chance, but I *hoped* . . ."

"Baby," he murmured. "You're soaking for me."

"Always," she said. "Quick. Take me."

He lifted her, propping her up on a high crate, bunching the skirt around her waist. The air felt cool against her damp thighs. He spread her pussy open with his fingertips, and she whimpered with desire, scooting to the edge of the box. He stepped forward: it was a perfect height for him to enter her. She wrapped her legs around his waist, drawing him in deeper, feeling his hard length fill her in one smooth, sharp motion. She tilted her head back, bucking her hips against him, her pussy clenching hard against his cock.

"*Beth.*" He withdrew slowly, then lunged forward, pressing up. His hand went between their bodies, stroking her clit, knowing just where to touch her. She cried out softly, then leaned forward, biting his shoulder to somehow muffle the sounds of her passion. Her fingers clawed at the small of his back, urging him even deeper inside her.

He seemed to understand. His thrusts were quick and deep, rocking inside her, stroking the flesh inside her cunt with strong, slightly circling motions that made her whole body thrum with pleasure.

She knew she ought to be listening. Anyone might come, walk in on them. They could be discovered. Strangely, instead of being afraid, the thought only heightened her acute sense of sexual arousal.

"God, you're so wet," he whispered, his breathing fast and sharp. "So fucking *tight*. I can feel your pussy milking my cock . . ."

She strained against him, climbing on him, lifting and lowering herself on his cock, meeting each thrust with perfect tempo until he finally lifted her from the crate, holding her against him, his muscular arms lifting her easily. She was breathing hard against his neck, shifting and rocking, feeling the ridge of his cock brushing against the hard knot of her clit and the sensitive outer flesh of her labia as he moved relentlessly against her.

The first orgasm surprised her, and she cried out. He kissed her, swallowing the sound as quickly as possible, and she shimmied, writhing with the ecstasy of it. He groaned, his pumping movements increasing in speed. The second and third orgasms lit her up like fireworks, and she screamed into his mouth as his powerful cock slammed home. He returned the favor with a guttural groan, holding her tight against his pelvis. She could feel his penis jerking inside her, and she tightened around him, her cunt quivering with the aftershocks of her multiple orgasms.

Slowly, he scooted forward, placing her gently back on the crate even as he was still buried inside her. The rush of blood in her head subsided. Frowning, she vaguely registered a sound she hadn't noticed in the heat of the moment.

"Do you hear that?"

He tilted his head, his breathing ragged. He held his breath, then frowned. "What is that?"

She went still, listening hard.

"It's the Bell of Hours," she said. "They're ringing it. It's too early . . . they shouldn't be ringing it."

She felt shock go through her. Ringing the Bell of Hours outside of the Founders' schedule meant only one thing.

Punishment.

Dread chilled her. "We have to go," she said.

He withdrew, leaving her wet, sticky, and with a perverse sense of disappointment, even though she had just had several orgasms from the man. *I'll get more later,* she thought. *I'll give more later.*

That is, assuming they weren't the ones being punished. That thought made bile rise in her throat. She quickly grabbed her veil, pulling it on, tucking all her hair safely away. "You have to leave, now," she said, as he did up his pants.

"When can I see you again?"

"Tonight," she said. "As long as . . ." She swallowed hard.

"As long as what?" He frowned. "Why is the bell ringing?"

"They'll want us to congregate at the Commons," she said instead, hedging. "I don't know why. Maybe it's a lecture."

But she knew, somehow, that it was something far darker. She just wasn't sure what.

Chapter Ten

Stephen took a roundabout route away from the Dining Hall, blending in to the chaotic crowd of men heading toward the Commons.

"What's going on?" Stephen asked Goodman Joshua, whose lumbering size made him easy to pick out of the crowd.

Joshua looked grim. "I have a bad feeling," he said, in his low voice, "that there's some sort of punishment."

Considering what he'd just been up to, Stephen felt a twinge of discomfort. "I thought punishment was rare," he said.

The thought crossed his mind: maybe it wouldn't be so bad if he and Beth got "caught," all things considered. If they were both banished, that would sort of neatly solve the problem—for him, anyway.

He immediately felt guilty even considering the possibility . . . but he considered it anyway.

The men around him were muttering to each other, conjecturing on what could have happened to create an unprecedented hiccup in the Founders' otherwise set-in-stone Bell of Hours scheduled routine. Obviously it was something bad, Stephen discovered. It was just a matter of how bad.

Women stood on one side of the Commons, men on the other, with an informal line of grass splitting between them. They were careful not to let the line thin too much, or get too close. Stephen couldn't see Beth, and he moved as close to the gender border as he dared.

From what he could discern from the conversations going on around him, the crowd was split between those who were excited at the unprecedented novelty, and those who were dismayed at what they were about to witness. Stephen found himself in the first camp, frankly curious at what might happen.

There was a raised dais at the end of the Commons . . . apparently in the summer, they held their weekly lectures there, before bedtime. But today was not a lecture. Amos looked somber, almost sad. Robert looked more vicious than usual. And Timothy, port, cherubic Timothy, looked like somebody had just put a big juicy hamburger in front of him. He was all but drooling over the prospect.

Suddenly, Stephen's curiosity diminished, and he switched his position. Whatever they were about to do, he got the feeling he didn't want to see it.

Founder Amos stepped forward. "Sisters and Brothers," he said, his booming voice needing no microphone to carry over the crowd. "There has been a vile transgression against the tenets of belief."

A thrilled shock jolted through the crowd, and the murmurs escalated.

"Goodmaids Lydia and Camille and Goodman Henry were found fornicating in the meadow by the dark woods," Founder Amos said. "We are quite certain this is not the first time. This behavior goes against everything the Penitents have sworn to turn away from. They have indulged in the sins of the flesh! They have reveled in the basest form of lust and carnality!"

The crowd gasped in unison.

Several of the other Founders dragged up the "transgressors." To Stephen's shock, they were naked. Their hands were bound, and there were burlap bags over their faces. Stephen felt his stomach churn.

Had he really once thought these people—the Founders, the Penitents—were harmless?

"What shall we do with these transgressors against our beliefs?" Founder Amos prompted.

It started as a low statement, then the crowd picked up the chant: "Punish them. Punish them! *Punish them!*"

"They will be punished," he said. "And they will be *banished.*"

A ragged cheer met this announcement.

"Tie them up," Founder Amos said dispassionately.

The Founders put up three posts, and the lovers were tied to them, Lydia in the center. Stephen watched in growing horror as they were caned across their bare backs, several lashes. They each cried out, writhing in agony, their nudity making it seem like some kind of grotesque fetish.

He glanced over at Joshua, certain that the gentle giant

would help him put a stop to the madness. Joshua was look-ing at his shoes.

Stephen leaned over, nudging him. "We can't just watch this," Stephen said.

"I'm not watching."

Stephen heard one of the women scream, and he nudged harder. "I mean, we have to stop this!"

Joshua finally looked at him, and his eyes were tortured. "We can't," he said softly. "Then they'll just kill us."

"Sure, we're outnumbered, but . . ." Joshua's words sank in. "Wait a minute. *Kill* us?"

Joshua glanced around nervously, but the rest of the crowd was too riveted on the spectacle playing out in front of them to notice. "The blood lust is on them," he said. "I've only seen it once before, and I've heard of worse incidents occur-ring . . ."

Stephen looked at the men standing around the two of them. They were staring up with pure hatred, many of them punching their fists in the air in time with the whistling lash. They looked mindless. They were a mob.

It wouldn't take much to push them over, he realized . . . or for them to decide to add a few bystanders for daring to interfere with necessary punishment.

Stephen clenched his jaw until he thought he'd break his teeth. It tore at him to stand aside while people were being hurt. Just when he thought he couldn't take it any more, the whipping stopped. The only sounds left were the hooded, naked people sobbing.

"And now," Founder Amos said, gesturing to Founder Robert, "for banishment."

Lydia screamed.

Stephen wondered why that should be so much worse than the beating. Were they so brainwashed, he thought, that they'd actually prefer to *stay* with these psychotic nut bags, than go out in the real world and take their chances?

Founder Roberts disappeared with a few of the others. They came back bearing three pine coffins.

"What the hell?" Stephen breathed.

They propped the coffins up. Then they untied Lydia, Camille, and Henry, and removed their hoods. Which meant that the lovers got to watch as they were shoved into the coffins. Their hands were still bound, as were their feet . . . so all they could do was wriggle helplessly, bashing against the sides of their boxes. Stephen could still hear them struggling as the Founders placed the lids on them and started to nail them shut.

"Please," Stephen said, sickness roiling through him, "please tell me that's ceremonial. That it's just some huge, metaphorical gesture that they're dead to the cult or something."

Joshua looked green. He shook his head slowly, and Stephen's stomach dropped.

"Banishment doesn't mean shunning, like it does in other sects," Joshua said, so softly Stephen could barely hear him. "It means death."

Beth retreated to the relative safety of her bedroom, still feeling shaken from what she'd just seen. She couldn't believe it, couldn't quite make sense of it.

She'd watched as the coffins were carried off, with their occupants still screaming, then loaded into the back of the old white Penitent van. She watched with the rest of the crowd as Founder Timothy drove off slowly, the van bumping down the long dirt road that led to the barbed-wire gate, slowly disappearing out of sight in the dense forest.

She'd heard about the dangers of banishment—they all had. It was whispered about every now and then, and the Founders would make lectures about it every year or so. But no one had ever spoken of it in detail. They only knew it was worse than being beaten, or confined, or starved: it was the worst punishment imaginable. People who had been in the camp for over fifteen years spoke of the last banishment with horror, but the Founders threatened anyone who spoke of it overtly—and apparently the banishment was terrifying enough to keep that silence. So it had taken on an almost mythic tone. After the horrors of the palace, Beth had shrugged off the rumors and the legends of the punishment: she knew what true terror was, and while she'd be disappointed if she got sent away from the camp, and desperate for the safety, she knew that there were worse things than simply being banished.

Now, she realized, she'd made a terrible miscalculation. Everything she'd been warned, everything she'd shrugged off, was worse than she could have even dreamed.

She'd stood there for long moments afterward, speechless, as if waiting for it all to prove to be some elaborate prank: as if the van would return, Lydia and Camille and Henry would be freed, and they'd promise not to do anything else. Then the Founders would send them to their respective dormitories without food for a few days. Put them on extra-hard cleaning detail.

After twenty minutes, she left with the rest of the straggling women, most of who were talking in hushed voices, salaciously imagining how *"three people"* might be having sex. At that point, Beth faced the inevitable. She knew instinctively that Lydia and Camille and Henry would not be freed. Now she digested the fact they would not leave those boxes. Not alive, at least.

She wondered absently if they'd be dead before the boxes were put in the ground.

The thought sent a frantic chill through her system. She'd thought she was safe here. And she was—from her step-mother, the Queen.

But who would save her from her saviors?

Of course, if she simply stayed on the straight and narrow, and obeyed all the tenets of belief, they'd have no cause to punish her. After all, no one had been banished in all the time she'd been there, and that was ten long years. There had been a few punishments, some random beatings, but she'd never seen anything like what she'd seen today.

Her eyes went to her bed frame. She had stowed the black lingerie she'd gotten from the delivery woman under her mattress.

What would the Founders do if they discovered that? She shivered.

Worse, what would they have done if someone had walked in on the little interlude she'd shared with Stephen in the pantry of the Dining Hall?

She broke out into a cold sweat at just how close to disaster she'd come.

So what now?

Stephen was supposed to see her tonight. She ought to send him a note, warning him away. It was too dangerous, for both of them.

Stephen was right. She had to make new choices.

She swallowed hard, staring out the window. The sun was setting. The Bell of Hours would be signaling dinner any moment.

What she should do, she realized, was tell Stephen to leave.

She closed her eyes. She had been strong enough to escape a deadly situation once. This place was not the sanctuary she'd tried to pretend it was. She was facing another life choice: remain, pretending to be something she wasn't, living half a life in the hopes of simply surviving . . . turning her back on the dangers of the outside world while leaping through hoops to avoid the dangers of the Compound.

And worst of all, walking away from the love of a man who would die for her.

Could you live without him?

She thought back to her days in the palace. When grief at her mother still clawed at her, and her father had offered no comfort. When the new Queen had started turning on her stepdaughter. When she'd turned her back on everything she'd ever known, to start a new life in the woods of Pennsylvania, away from her past and her old self. When she'd killed Bianca and became reborn as Goodmaid Beth.

She could live without Stephen, if she had to. She knew that.

But I don't want to.

There was a knock at her door, and she looked up, uncomfortably surprised. She was expecting no one.

After today's events, she did not like surprises.

She opened the door. When she discovered who was there, she was shocked.

"Founder Amos," she said, quickly looking to the floor. "You're . . . you're in the women's dormitory."

It was unheard of.

"It's unfortunate, but after the Lydia situation," and his voice sounded distasteful, as if he'd swallowed a sour grape, "the Founders are investigating the women's dormitory. We can be trusted to negotiate the exposure to the opposite gender. Besides, we all must do our part and face . . . certain unpleasantries, shall we say, in the name of the greater good."

"Of course," Beth murmured, barely listening to him. She suddenly thought back to the lingerie, and began to sweat.

"I wanted to speak to you privately," Founder Amos said . . . then he crossed the room, shocking her further by sitting on her bed. She tried not to stare at the spot that concealed the contraband underclothing, but couldn't stare at his face. She stood at the opposite corner of the room, feeling trapped. "Before . . . the unfortunate incident earlier, Lydia mentioned that you were aware of what was going on. She even suggested that you might also be involved in transgressions . . . of a similar nature."

Beth felt the cold brush of fear. Then control, paired with icy resolve, cloaked her. It was just like being in the palace, she realized.

It had been years, but she'd survived then. She would, for damned certain, survive now.

She met his probing gaze. "Did she?" Beth said, her voice surprised and irritated. "With whom?"

"She didn't know." He didn't blink. Neither did Beth. Finally, he smiled. "I knew it. She hated you. Your face definitely creates some problems, doesn't it?"

Beth sighed. "It's part of why I came here." Which was true enough. Her stepmother had hated her face. She resembled her mother too closely.

Founder Amos stood, stepping close to her, and Beth felt trapped for an entire other reason. He didn't touch her, but the way he was looking at her felt just as invasive. "Your face is a temptation," he mused. "Many men stare at you, and just looking at you—your eyes, your lips—they're led to start thinking of temptation and impurities." He paused. "Sexual . . . impurities."

Her stomach turned.

"It's not your fault, though," he said. "I've noticed several of the men staring at you over the years."

Beth shrugged, unsure of what to say. "I do not invite their attention."

"No, of course you don't," he said, his voice meant to be reassuring. He sounded like the charismatic, fatherly man she'd always known . . . but his eyes still gleamed salaciously, and he looked at her body in a way that made her skin crawl.

Had he always felt this way? And if he had . . . why was he showing her now?

"It's also natural for a woman like you to be . . . well, curious," Founder Amos said.

Now she felt like she'd been hit by a train. "Lust is a transgression against the tenets of belief," she rattled off, out of sheer nervousness.

"Sometimes," he said, and his voice went low, "you need to get to truly know the temptation in order to purge it."

He started to reach for her. She jerked back, crossing her arms in front of her. "Would the other Founders see it that way, I wonder?"

Now he was the one to step back. He glared at her.

"I see." His voice was cold. "I was offering to . . . help you get to know the nature of your temptation. But perhaps there is someone else in the Compound that has caught your eye?"

She didn't look at him. She couldn't look at him.

"Well, I know of one Newcomer who has been attracted to you. He's slavered after you. It's disgusting," the Founder spat out. "But not to worry, my dear. I can guarantee you won't be subjected to his lusting any more."

Now she looked at him. "What are you talking about?"

"It's happened a few times before. There were other men. Other occasions of . . . inappropriate interest," he said. "Don't worry. I will take care of it personally."

With that, he walked to the door, turning to her, his face as mild as if they'd just discussed the weather. "Get ready, child. Dinner will be ringing soon."

He left.

She stared at the door, still uncomprehending. He'd threatened Stephen, that she felt quite sure of. But what did he mean, *he'd take care of it personally?*

Suddenly, she recalled other incidents . . . men staring at

her, early on, when she had just come to the camp. Then the men disappearing. She'd thought they had just left the group. One had died in a mining incident, she recalled.

She now realized it was no accident.

Cold chills consumed her.

She had to warn Stephen, before it was too late.

Chapter Eleven

Stephen crept toward the women's dormitory. He needed to get the hell out of here—get the police involved, do something. Three people had been murdered, for God's sake, or were in the process of. He was probably too late for Henry and Lydia and Camille, but he couldn't just pretend nothing had happened. And he certainly couldn't wait for things to get worse.

As always, his first thought had been of Beth. He didn't care how "safe" she might feel here; they were psychotic, and she was in danger. Which meant he was getting her out of this insane asylum, too.

He just needed to figure out how.

A hand touched his shoulder, and he spun, his fists primed, his whole body tensed to strike.

"It's me," Beth whispered, and he felt relief flood through him.

"Jesus, you scared me," he hissed back, lowering his hands.

"Hurry," she said. "It's not safe."

He followed her into the darkness of the woods, stumbling on exposed tree roots and dead branches. The place had seemed so nice and idyllic when he'd first gotten here. Now, every shadow looked menacing, and the trees themselves seemed to reach out and grab at their clothing. It was like a haunted wood, or something. The sliver of moon barely lit their way.

She avoided the meadow, heading instead for a thicket of dense bushes, and a nestled hollow. A few of the branches scratched his arms and neck as he forced his way past.

"They won't be able to see us here," she murmured, close to his ear. "The thorn bushes are too thick, and the Founders generally watch the perimeter. I don't know how they caught Lydia, or where, so . . ."

"So the meadow was out," he whispered back. "Beth, we've got to get out of here."

"I know," she said.

He blinked, startled. "Really?"

She stared back at him. "I couldn't believe they'd murder them . . . Lydia, and Camille, and Henry," she said. "I didn't *want* to believe it. But now I know what they're capable of. We can't stay here. I know that now."

He nodded. "We've got to get to the police," he said. "But first, we have to leave this Compound."

She sighed, sitting down on the springy grass. He sat next to her, putting an arm around her, trying to comfort her. She looked shell-shocked. "It won't be easy," she said. "There's the barbed-wire fence . . . and women aren't allowed out of the Compound, for any reason."

He frowned. "There's got to be a way . . ."

"There is," she said slowly, taking a deep breath. "You've got to get out first."

"And leave you behind?" His whole body reacted to the appalling thought. "No fucking way."

"Think this through," she said. "The Founders trust me. They like me." She swallowed hard. "Apparently, Founder Amos likes me . . . a great deal."

Now he was aghast. "What did he do to you?"

"Nothing," she said, putting a hand on his arm, now comforting him. "But . . . I get the feeling he's got plans for me. . . ."

"And you expect me to just leave you here with that monster? Alone, unprotected?"

"What can you do to protect me?" she asked, her voice cool and logical, even though her blue eyes were sad. "Nothing. You can't protect me here. You can't help me."

The thought nauseated him. "Bullshit. There's always something."

"You can get out," she said. "He knows you're interested in me. He mentioned that he would take care of anyone who was interested in me." She was so pale, her skin was almost translucent. "He hinted that he had in the past. A mining accident. You've got to be careful."

Stephen almost wished they would try something, but he knew that was just defenses and ego, bristling, eager for action. He'd love to hurt the people who were threatening him and the woman he'd fallen in love with. "There's got to be another way," he protested. "You've been here ten years. You mean to say that nobody has ever tried escaping before?"

Beth shrugged. "Men have left on occasion," she said, "usually because it was easier for them to do so. Women . . ." She shivered. "We had a few attempts to leave. Goodmaid Jessica tried to get over the fence. Her clothes got caught on the barbed wire. She's the one with the scars on her face and arms. That's to say nothing of the beating she received after she was caught."

Stephen recoiled, aghast.

"Normally, when a woman is that unhappy," Beth continued somberly, "she escapes the only way she can." She paused. "The usual method is hanging herself."

Stephen felt his stomach sink.

"When you leave for your off-Compound work, do whatever you can to get away from them," she continued. "I've got an idea on how to get myself out."

"How?" He didn't like the way this plan was working: too much was out of his control, and the thought of leaving Beth, even for a short time, in the hands of these madmen was both cowardly and appalling. But she seemed to be the more reasonable of the two of them tonight.

"The same way I got the condoms, and the lingerie," she said. "There's a delivery woman who brings in our food order. Lydia had an arrangement. I'm going to see if I can get her to agree to smuggle me out."

"I don't know," Stephen said. "It's one thing to sneak in little things. It's another to help a person escape."

"I know," Beth said, "but it's my only option."

Stephen sat, silent, struggling against the inevitability of this solution. He had no way to get her out on his own. Even if he stole a vehicle, they'd be stopped by the damned gate, which was deliberately heavy and operated by guards. The fences were high, topped with barbed wire. He might be able to make it over, but there would be guards watching the fences, he knew it. They'd already tapped several of the Goodmen to walk the perimeter, "just to make sure no one got uneasy over the afternoon's activities." They would be extra cautious. And if Beth and he were caught trying to escape . . .

He shuddered at the thought.

"You know I'm right," Beth said.

"I don't like it," he said, his voice hoarse. "I don't like leaving you here."

She stroked his face, and he held her tight, crushing her against his chest. "I know you don't like it," she whispered against his neck. "I love that you want to protect me. I haven't felt that in so long . . ."

He leaned down and kissed her fiercely, terrified at the thought of losing her, now that he'd found her. "Why you?" he murmured against her lips. "Why did I have to find you here? Why do you mean so much to me?"

"I love you," she whispered back. "I'm glad you found me."

"I don't know what I'd do if anything happened to you."

"Nothing's going to happen," she murmured. "We'll be safe. We'll be together."

He kissed her harder, emotions churning through him.

She reached for him hungrily, meeting his kiss with a heated passion of her own. He couldn't help himself. He reached for her, tugging at the material of her nightgown, and she pulled the hem up willingly, stripping off her white cotton panties. She undid the button fly of his pants, ripping them open, tugging the material down enough for his cock to emerge, hard and eager. He reached for her breasts, caressing them, sucking them through the thick cloth of her nightgown, and she tugged the gown over her head, leaving her gloriously naked. He tore off his shirt, tossing it beneath them, next to her gown. He pulled her on top of him, and she spread her legs, eagerly. He nudged the soft flesh of her thighs, the silky skin stroking his cock, moistening it with the dew of her already slick pussy. He pressed against her damp curls, and she sighed, kissing his mouth.

He pushed in, just the tip, before realizing he hadn't brought any protection. He'd been too intent on their escape to think they'd have a chance to make love, but now, with the possibility that one or both of them might get hurt—or worse—making love with her at least one last time was all he could think about.

"Damn," he muttered, trying to force himself to pull back. It wasn't fair!

"No," she protested, pushing down, drawing his cock inside her hot, wet warmth, burying the head of him inside her. "I want you."

"Baby, I didn't bring a condom . . ." he whispered, trying to ignore the phenomenal feel of her, naked and pulsing against him. "Don't, Beth, sweetheart . . . it's not . . ."

"I don't care," she said sharply. "We don't know what's going to happen next. I want you inside me. I want everything you can give me. *I want you.*"

He gave in, gritting his teeth. She lowered herself onto his erect cock with maddening slowness, sighing with bliss as her cunt took him in, inch by inch. The feeling defied words. He hadn't been naked inside a woman in years, and the feel of her, pulsating around him, her body hot and milking him like a fist, was mind blowing. He groaned as she moved with infinitesimal slowness.

"This feels . . . so different," she said, and her voice had a quality of wonder in it. "So much *nicer* . . ."

Nicer. Understatement of the millennium. He leaned back against their crumpled clothes and the damp, thick grass, pulling her against him, feeling her body contract against him as she leaned forward. Her breasts crushed against his chest. "Just stay like this for a second," he said, breathless as a marathon runner. "I want to remember this. I want to remember you like this."

She smiled at him, a tender smile that destroyed him. She kissed him, her tongue tickling at the edges of his lips, then coaxed his tongue with her own. He obliged, growling with pleasure. The feel of his tongue in her mouth and his cock in her pussy was overwhelming, and he clutched her to him, gripping her buttocks, pressing her body so close to his that he couldn't tell where she began and he ended.

Then she started to squirm, deliciously, her breathing going shallow. "I want you," she whispered, between heated kisses against his chest. She propped herself up, straddling him, her thighs cradling his cock. She smiled, swiveling her hips slightly. He groaned at the intensity of the sensation, his hips lifting her. She laughed softly.

It seemed like all his senses were heightened. He could smell the damp grass, the distant hint of rain in the humid air, the thick scent of honeysuckle carrying on the slight breeze. He could hear the babble of the stream, the hushed rustling of the branches of the trees. And above all, he could sense *her*: the sweet-flower scent of her, the satin of her skin, the silk of her hair, the wet heat of her core. The music of her voice.

He couldn't get enough of this woman. He would be obsessed with her until the day he died.

"Stephen," she murmured, her hips beginning to pick up speed. She rose up on her knees, causing him to withdraw slowly, and he raised his hips to try and bury himself back inside her. She obliged, pressing down, enveloping him completely in her pussy, the wet juices of their pleasure cascading down his balls. He tugged at her hips, pressing deeper within her folds, and she tilted her body backward, forcing the tip of his cock against her G-spot. She started to move, harder now, with more force. Her breasts jutted forward, nipples erect, and her eyes were closed, her lashes a thick dark fringe against the creamy paleness of her skin. Her full red lips were parted in an expression of blooming ecstasy, as she rode him mindlessly toward completion.

He could feel the beginnings of her orgasm, the wet rush flooding over him, the way her muscles rippled around his penis, and he moved faster, knowing what she liked. The first wave hit, and the clenching of her pussy was more than he could deny: he gave in, answering her release with his own. He emptied himself into her, his body wracking with the most powerful orgasm he'd ever felt. He groaned, and she slammed her body against his, their pelvises bucking together in a frenzy of passionate need.

When it was over, she collapsed against his chest, breathing hard, her body still shivering and contracting with the aftershocks of her pleasure. He felt each minute pulse, marveling at the contact.

It was probably stupid: they had no protection. But he trusted her. He loved her. If their passion tonight bore fruit . . . if a child were the result . . .

He closed his eyes. He wanted it to be her. He wanted a future with her in it.

He held her tightly to him, almost afraid of what might happen.

"We'll be all right," she whispered again, comforting him.

Still, he didn't let her go.

It was getting late, and she knew that she had to let him go . . . that every second they were away from the dormitories, they were in danger. Founder Amos was already targeting Stephen, and she didn't need to give them any more reason to hurt either Stephen or herself.

But she cuddled against him, her skin warmed by the heat of

his body. She didn't want to leave him. Especially when there were so many unknowns, so many uncertainties. She hadn't felt this afraid since she'd planned her "death," all those many years ago, back on the island of Iko, her home kingdom.

"We have to go," he murmured, nuzzling her neck.

"Not quite yet," she said, her voice sounding sleepy. "I just want a little more of you."

"I would've thought you'd had enough," he teased softly.

"Never." She could still feel the sticky wetness of their coupling, between her legs . . . smell the scent of their sex, mingling with the smells of summer and the woods. "I don't think I'll ever get enough of you."

She felt his erection starting to grow, and she reached down, circling the flagging flesh with her fingers. She squeezed softly, then more firmly, feeling him respond by growing beneath her probing touch.

"Beth," he breathed.

"Quickly," she said. "Just once. Then we'll go, I promise."

"Quickly," he said, spooning behind her.

She got on her knees, cushioned by her gown and his shirt. He got behind her on his knees, his legs between hers. He spread the cheeks of her buttocks, stroking the length of her with his cock head. She shivered in response, then cried out softly as he nudged the hard knot of her clit. She looked over her shoulder to see him lick his finger, then he replaced his cock with his hand, stroking her, piercing her.

"Oh," she gasped, pressing against him. "More. I want more of you."

"Beth." His voice was a caress. She could feel the full hard length of him inside her, pushing into her, filling her. She bucked against him, and he held her hips tight, thrusting with increasing speed and force. She leaned back, arching, squeezing her buttocks and thighs tight, feeling her body close around his hot, hard flesh. She gasped as he slid inside her and withdrew, moving with utmost skill.

He reached around, cupping one breast with one hand and then stroking her clit with the other. The two of them were kneeling, writhing against each other, and she threw her head back against his chest, rocking against him, feeling the overwhelming sensation of his hands on her nipple and her clit and his cock buried tight in her pussy, and she wanted to scream as pleasure ravaged her system. But he wasn't done with her. He turned her to face him, and she wrapped her legs around him as he lifted and lowered her, clutching her in a hug as his buttocks clenched and his abdomen worked, straining to make each measured thrust count.

Another orgasm shot through her, and she bit his shoulder, then licked his collarbone. "I want you to come inside me," she said, her voice hoarse, her breathing short. "I want to feel you come, all hot and wet and pounding inside me . . ."

He groaned. "Beth, baby, I want you . . ."

"Then take me," she whispered. "Fuck me, Stephen. I want you to fuck me *so hard* . . ."

It pushed him over the edge. He slammed into her, and she felt the shock of his thrust against her clit and her G-spot, in turn sending her spiraling into the abyss. She could feel the hot spurt of his semen inside her, as her pussy clenched and contracted against his shuddering cock.

She still held him, unwilling to let go, raining kisses on his collarbone, his neck, his face. He kissed her back, tender, hungry, stroking her flesh, keeping himself embedded inside her. It was as if the two of them couldn't bear to let each other go.

Finally, they separated, reluctantly putting on their clothes. "I'll leave tomorrow," he said, his voice slow and heavy. "When we get to the mine. I'll figure out a way to duck out and make a break for it."

She nodded. "I'll see if I can get the delivery woman to help me escape," she said.

"If you can't," he said, "the first place I'm going is to the police. I'm sure they'll help me out. If nothing else, I'll tell them you're in danger and want to leave."

She nodded. "All right," she said, feeling uneasy. If the police got involved, she'd have to say who she was . . . they'd want identification. Which she didn't have. And, if pressed . . . wouldn't they find out she was the Princess?

She would worry about that tomorrow.

When they were fully dressed, they left the thicket. He pressed one last kiss against her lips. "I want you to do something for me," he said.

She nodded.

"Remember this cell phone number." He rattled off a number, several times, then had her repeat it. "That's my number. I can check messages anywhere, and I'll get my phone back as soon as I get finished with the cops. If you get out before I contact them, call me, all right? Then I'll come and get you."

"All right."

He stroked her hair, then kissed her, long and lingering. "Whatever else, just make sure you're safe," he said. "I couldn't bear it if anything happened to you."

She smiled, feeling cherished. Feeling loved.

"See you soon," he said, disappearing back into the darkened forest. She could hear his muffled footsteps, heading off toward the men's dormitory.

"See you soon," she echoed softly, then headed back to wait for tomorrow.

Chapter Twelve

"I'm telling you," Stephen said to the policeman for the third time, "they put these people in coffins. They were going to kill them."

The policeman sighed. Stephen knew that it was hard to take him seriously, considering his clothes. But the guy didn't have to be such a prick about it.

"Did you see these people being harmed?"

"I saw them being beaten," Stephen said with a grimace. "I saw them being nailed into coffins. Isn't that enough?"

"Then what happened?"

"They loaded the coffins up in a van," Stephen explained. "Then the van drove away."

"Drove away where?"

"I don't know," Stephen said. "I couldn't follow them. I was trapped, myself."

"Were you physically restrained?"

"Not exactly," he admitted. "But . . . well, their fence has barbed wire at the top of it. It's basically a prison."

The policeman sighed. "Hold on," he said. "I've got somebody you should talk to."

Stephen sat, getting more and more impatient. The longer he dicked around with these guys, the more worried he got about Beth. The Founders obviously meant business. If they ever found out what he and Beth were up to . . . hell, they apparently didn't even need evidence. Timothy was willing to rub him out on Amos's say-so. A "mining accident."

Stephen wondered how many accidents were caused by Penitent politics.

A man with graying hair and a sharp-looking suit walked up to him. "You're Stephen Trent?" he asked. His voice was gruff, at odds with his sophisticated style. "You came in with the complaint about the Penitents?"

Stephen nodded, standing.

"I'm Lieutenant Grady," the man said, offering his hand. Stephen shook it. "Come with me."

Grady led him to a small room. It was probably an interrogation room, Stephen thought, wondering if he'd gotten himself in more trouble somehow. "Am I going to need a lawyer?" he said, half joking.

"No, nothing like that," Grady said, sighing heavily. "They referred you to me because I've been following the Penitents for a few years now. Generally, they're considered harmless. As far as cults go, anyway. We're not talking Jonestown or that Waco fiasco. They're just a bunch of back-to-the-simple-life junkies." Grady's face darkened. "At least, that's what they've always been portrayed as. But I've got a disappear-ance from about twelve years ago that has ties to them, and there have been some complaints from families about sons or daughters who have gone in and never come out, if you get my meaning."

Stephen nodded. He'd written stories about cults before. He knew that there wasn't anything you could legally do, if your family member was old enough to make his own deci-sions. You just had to tough it out.

"I've spoken with their leader. That Amos guy," Grady said, leaning back in his chair. "He's charming. Slick. Just a little too smug."

"You should meet Robert," Stephen said.

"That's the enforcer, huh? Big guy, maybe six two, heavy-set. Looks like he could bench an engine block." Grady nodded. "The whole crew seems loopy, but those two . . ."

"They seem dangerous," Stephen finished.

"You understand." Grady leaned forward now, his eyes alight. "You don't understand how tough it is to nail these guys. On the surface, they're clean as an operating table, but I've had too many dead ends and too many coincidences that point to them. I know they're dirty, and they're hiding some-thing. I just need proof."

Stephen sighed. "Well, I know that they're keeping people there against their will. Women aren't allowed to leave." He paused. "There's a woman there who I know wants to leave, but she can't."

"Well, we can go in there, get her out," Grady said.

"They'll see you coming," Stephen said. "They may claim she simply isn't there. Can you get a warrant or something?"

"Depends. Are you a relative?"

"No," Stephen said. *I'm her lover. Does that count?*

"So, all I've got is the word of a stranger that there's a woman in there, being held against her will." Grady rubbed his hand over his chin. "Pretty thin."

"I saw them nail a bunch of people into coffins," Stephen snapped. "Jesus Christ, what does it take to get you guys to act around here?"

"I've gone myself, on a report of the coffin thing. Years ago. It's supposed to be a ceremonial thing. Metaphorical. At least that's what they explained." Grady sounded tired, frustrated. "They produced people who said that they were simply banished . . . that the Founders brought the coffins out of the Compound, then released them. But considering how quickly they produced these 'banished' people, and how helpful they were . . ."

"You don't buy it."

"No, I don't," Grady said. "Damn it. They've got to slip up sometime."

"In the meantime, Beth's stuck there, with those lunatics," Stephen said sharply. "What can I do?"

Grady stood up, handing him a business card.

"I'm sure you'll keep an eye on the situation," he said, his voice grim. "You can give me a call the minute that they do something wrong."

"And what if that something is them killing the woman I love?" Stephen asked sarcastically.

"Then you'd better dial fast," Grady said. "That's the best I can do."

* * *

"Beth!"

Beth jumped, the broom she was holding falling from her hands and dropping to the floor. Goodmaid Cynthia frowned at her.

"Well, aren't you jumpy?" she asked, but was too intent on her gossip to study Beth's odd reaction. "Didn't mean to startle you, but did you hear?"

Beth's stomach fell sickeningly. "Hear what?"

"In the mines," Cynthia drew out. "There's been an incident."

Now nausea churned through her. "An . . . accident?" she clarified, hearing Founder Amos's voice in her head.

I will take care of it personally.

Other accidents, she thought. She wanted to scream at Cynthia, force her to tell her if anything had happened to Stephen. Instead, she kept silent.

"No, not an accident," Cynthia said impatiently. "An *incident*. One of the Goodmen left!"

Beth blinked. "What do you mean?"

"It's all the talk," Cynthia said, fluttering with excitement. "Founder Timothy came back in a sweat, and now all the Founders have left the Compound. They're bringing all the Goodmen back from the mine early! All because one man ran away!"

Beth felt her stomach slowly unknot. Her limbs felt suddenly light, and she felt almost dizzy with relief. "Do you know which man?" she asked.

Cynthia shook her head. "Can you imagine? Do you think it's because of . . ." she lowered her voice, looking around to see if anyone else was listening, "the . . . banishment?"

Banishment. So people were still **hanging on** to the euphemism.

"Probably," Beth said, forcing her voice to remain neutral. But she couldn't help it. "Didn't it bother you?"

"Didn't what bother me?"

"The banishment," Beth answered, still using the inaccurate label.

Cynthia shrugged, looking uncomfortable. "They had broken the tenets of belief," she said, looking a little unsure. "They were having sex. *All* of them." She lowered her voice, her expression shocked yet somewhat titillated. "*Together! At the same time!*"

"I know," Beth said, thinking ruefully of just how well she knew.

"That's obscene. Perverse." Cynthia tossed her head, making her veil shift. If she were a debutante, Beth could imagine her tossing her blond locks in a gesture of frivolity. "They knew the rules. They deserved what they got."

"They deserved *death*?"

Cynthia's expression slipped, exposing a look of fear. Then she stubbornly set her jaw.

"Nobody got killed," she said firmly. "They just . . . the coffins . . . they're for effect. We didn't *see* anybody get killed."

Beth looked at Cynthia with pity. "You don't believe that," she said quietly.

Cynthia huffed. "I see you're in no mood to talk," she said sourly, and left the kitchen, looking for more people to spread her exciting news. Beth finished cleaning, then stood in the pantry, feeling the harsh beating of her heart. She tried to breathe slowly, forcing herself to calm down.

Stephen is safe.

It was enough to buoy her in what lay ahead. As long as she knew Stephen had not been hurt or killed by the Founders, she could do what she needed to do.

"Hello there, girlie," the delivery woman said, hobbling into the kitchen, her arms full of a sack of oatmeal. "A little help, if you please."

Beth immediately began to unload the provisions.

"Where's Lydia?" the delivery woman asked, looking around. "Not like her to miss a shipment. I have a few items that she special ordered."

"Lydia . . ." Beth began. "She . . . isn't here anymore."

The other woman's eyes widened. "I thought none of you people ever left."

"There's one way," Beth muttered uncomfortably. "She got banished."

"Huh. Got caught, then." The woman shook her head. "Idiot. If you're going to keep a secret, you've got to play your cover to the core. She never should've come to a place like this."

The woman's callous attitude stung. "What would you know about it?"

"Oh, more than you think, dearie, more than you think. So, what about you?" She turned to Beth, the full scrutiny of that deformed face almost enough to make Beth flinch, but she was too angry and too intent to be swayed. "Have you learned your lesson, or are you still going to be a 'customer' of mine from now on? Because I brought something that I think you'd be very interested in . . ." She cackled a laugh.

Beth gritted her teeth. "I need your help," she said, in a low voice.

The cackling laughter stopped. "Help with what, now?"

"I need to get out of here," Beth said, even softer, looking carefully around. "I need your help to escape."

The cackle came back. "And I thought Lydia was ballsy," she said, her breath coming out in a wheeze. "Now that I can't do. It'd cost me my job, helping one of you get out. You're not supposed to leave the Compound. Even I know that."

"Don't you understand? *They killed Lydia.* For doing things with the products *you* got for her," Beth said. "Don't you feel at all guilty?"

"She knew what she was getting into," the woman said easily.

"She didn't know she'd be killed," Beth countered. "And I don't want to be killed."

"This isn't my business," the woman said, starting to pull away.

"There's a man," Beth said. "On the outside. He's going to help me. They won't need to know that you were a part of it, just like they didn't know about your arrangement with Lydia. The Founders are all out of the Compound today anyway. By the time they figure out it was you, I'll make sure you get enough money that you can get another job. All right?" When the woman made no response, Beth continued. "I'm begging you. Please. Please help me."

Beth could've sworn she saw the smallest gleam in the woman's rheumy blue eyes.

"I'm not made of stone," she finally said. "All right. If we do this, we have to do this fast . . . and do it now, before they get back."

Beth stood up straight. She had nothing to take with her—and nothing to leave behind. "Just tell me where to go."

The woman nodded to the inside of the van. "Get behind those boxes. They shouldn't shift around too much. Pull some moving blankets over you." She laughed, that dry, wheezy sound. "I haven't been searched yet, but if things have been happening the way you say, I wouldn't be surprised. Better safe than sorry."

Beth didn't need to be told twice. No one was watching—at least, no one that she could see. She would be gone before anyone knew she was missing.

She'd worry about the possibilities of being found out as the Princess later. Right now, she had only one goal: getting off the Compound and back with Stephen. She clambered into the storage part of the truck, ducked behind the boxes, and arranged the blankets around her.

"All right, here we go." The woman closed the truck with a slam, and Beth was plunged into darkness. She heard the engine rev up with a roar and felt the truck lumber forward.

The boxes moved plenty, she discovered, fighting not to be crushed as they jostled and slid with the slow momentum of the truck's driving. She was pummeled by them, unsure of what was going to hit her from where in the darkness. At least it distracted her from the tomblike feelings of claustrophobia that the stuffy compartment created.

Beth felt the bumps of the dirt road switch to the smooth ride of paved highway, and she breathed easier. They were out of the Compound. She was that much closer, to Stephen and to freedom.

She continued on in darkness for an indeterminable amount of time. Then, the truck pulled off the road, grinding to a halt. The truck's back door opened, and Beth blinked against the unaccustomed light.

They were at a motel, someplace small and seedy looking. Beth thought it looked like the Taj Mahal.

"All right, here's your stop," the delivery woman said gruffly.

How long had they been driving? Beth wondered how close she was to the Compound. Would it be far enough away?

Of course, what could the Founders do, outside of the Compound, or the mine?

"What about that money you promised me?"

Beth bit her lip. "I don't have it . . . now," she said. "I need to call someone. I need him to get to me."

"All right." The woman wrote down a phone number, handed it to her. Then she looked at Beth intently. "You don't have any money, do you? No ID, either?"

Beth shook her head, feeling miserable.

"God. I must be a softie," the woman grumbled. "You wait here."

Beth stood at the back of the truck, feeling out of place and conspicuous in her dark dress as women in jeans and sherbet-colored tank-tops walked out of hotel room doors, staring at her. Beth hadn't counted on this. She hadn't thought of much beyond getting away from the Compound. She reached up, feeling the veil still on her head. She probably looked like some kind of nun.

The delivery woman came back, handing Beth a key. "You're in room eighteen."

Beth stared at the key, tears of gratitude prickling at her eyes. "Why?"

"Do I know?" the woman grumbled. "You're going to need a place to lie low while your man comes to get you. I imagine he's probably on the run, too. So you two are gonna need a place to get your shit together. Might as well be here. I'll be back tomorrow to get my money."

Beth nodded, taking the woman's hand gratefully. "Thank you," she whispered. "So much. I can't thank you enough for your kindness to me."

The woman looked appalled, pulling her hand away. "Don't get all mushy on me," she said, but she sounded shaken. "Oh, that reminds me. I did get you something."

"You've done so much . . ." Beth protested, but the woman rummaged through the boxes, pulling out a small paper bag. She handed it to Beth, and Beth opened it.

It was a set of lingerie, cherry red and lacy and barely there. There was a bra and a scant pair of panties. The panties had an apple embroidered on the front, complete with a green leaf. It looked glossy and perfect.

"Forbidden fruit," the woman said. "Ha! Ironic, huh?"

"I couldn't . . ." Beth started to say, then thought briefly about what Stephen's expression would be, if he saw her in the skimpy outfit. She felt herself stir, growing wet at the mere daydream.

She would have him to herself, she thought.

"You want it," the delivery woman said. "Keep it. You can

pay me more, if you're still feeling guilty. Now, go on. You stand out more than I do—and that's saying somethin'."

Beth started to thank her again, but the woman was already turned and headed back to the cab of the truck. "Just remember," she added, hanging her head out of the window before she started the engine. "I'll be back here tomorrow for my money. Don't go anywhere."

"All right," Beth said, waving. Then she turned, taking the key and heading for room eighteen. She took off her veil, then picked up the phone and dialed Stephen's cell phone number.

"Hello?" she heard his voice, crackling with static.

"Stephen," she said, her voice full of emotion. "I'm free."

Chapter Thirteen

Stephen arrived at the motel room with a growing sense of excitement and anxiety. He'd been frantic, until he got Beth's call. Now, all he wanted was to get his arms around her and reassure himself that she was out and she was safe.

He knocked on her door, his penis already erect at the mere thought of Beth waiting on the other side. No more hiding. No more quick, furtive couplings in bathhouses or meadows or thickets. A real bed, he thought with a satisfied sigh, not some narrow camp cot.

The door opened slowly, revealing no one. The room itself was darkened, the curtains drawn.

Immediately his body tensed with a sense of foreboding. He took a step in, his hands starting to bunch in fists. The door shut behind him.

His breath caught in his throat.

"Hi, Stephen." Beth took a step forward, with a small, shy smile. She was wearing a matching set of bra and panties, all in a luscious, bright shade of crimson that glowed like a ripe cherry skin against the pale translucence of her skin. The demitasse cups of the bra pushed her breasts up to their best advantage, and his mouth watered looking at the perky roundness that was just begging for him to taste them. He could barely make out the rosy curve of her nipples, peeking out through the edging lace.

His gaze wandered lower, hypnotically. The panties were French cut, riding high on her thighs in thin wisps of lace. The triangle of red at the juncture of her thighs was an enticing little swath of satin. And sitting just below her navel, like an invitation, was an embroidered apple, red with a hint of green, topped with a glossy leaf.

Temptation, he thought. He traced the fruit with his thumb.

She let out an explosive sigh. "I can't believe you're here," she murmured. Then she laughed. "I can't believe I'm here. It all seems . . . unreal."

"I know," he said, cradling her tenderly, even as his body started to ignite with the passion that had been growing since the first moment he'd laid eyes on this woman. "We're free, Beth. We can go wherever we want, do whatever we want." With his hand, he stroked the flat plane of her stomach, letting his fingertips brush behind the apple, barely touching the top of the curls of her sex. "Take as long as we want," he said, his voice husky.

"That sounds good," she whispered. "It's like the first time, all over again."

He leaned his head against her shoulder, pressing small, suckling kisses against her neck, reveling in the sound of her small gasps. "It'll be like the first time," he promised. "Better than the first time."

He tugged gently at her hand, leading her to the bed. Her hand trembled as she reached for the waistband of his T-shirt, tugging at it. He took it off slowly, tossing it to the floor. Then he hugged her, lightly, a teasing brush of skin on skin. The smooth texture of her bra was no competition to the rose petal softness of her skin; the feel of her seduced him as his bare chest slid against her. She leaned up, kissing his collarbone, her round nails delicately clawing down the planes of his abdomen . . . then inching lower, undoing the top button of his fly.

His cock strained against the denim of his jeans, but he did nothing to rush her. She inched the zipper down, then pushed his clothing aside with infinite care. His erection sprang free as she edged his jeans and boxers down past his knees. He kicked off his shoes and socks, letting his pants fall the rest of the way. He was now completely naked, and trembling with need for her.

The room was simple, bare but clean, in the way of most inexpensive motels. To Stephen, it felt as regal as a palace because she was there. He kissed her, nudging her toward the bed. He leaned down, his hands barely holding her waist as he kissed her mouth with exquisite care, his tongue tracing the satiny softness of her lips before tickling their way inside, mating with her tongue in teasing, light strokes. His cock tightened almost painfully as he felt a burst of sugary warmth unfurl in the pit of his stomach.

God, I love this woman.

He stroked her hair, breathing hard. Her long black locks looked like a waterfall of onyx. Her long fringe of black lashes framed her violet blue eyes, which seemed to gleam in the dim light of the motel room as she peered up at him. She stretched out. "The bed's so big," she said. She laughed, delighted, then stretched out her arms and legs, as if making snow angels. Stephen laughed with her. "So much room."

"I'm sure we'll find a way to use it," he promised, sliding next to her.

He kissed her slowly, his mouth working on hers, teasing her, tempting her. She kissed him back, and he felt it like a warm bath, seeping slowly into his tense muscles, making his entire body feel hot and at the same time relaxed and rejuvenated.

Making love to her was like coming home, he realized. More than any home he'd ever known.

He worked his way down, his tongue tracing a meandering path down the valley of her deliciously presented cleavage. She moaned softly, her back arching in invitation. He licked at her nipples through the lacy fabric, the way he knew she liked. She cried out, a muted shriek.

"You can be as loud as you like," he murmured against her hot skin.

"What . . . what about our neighbors?" she whispered back, sounding scandalized.

He lifted his head, grinning at her shocked expression. "A motel like this," he said, "I'm sure they're used to it."

She looked doubtful. He'd just have to show her, he thought, and his grin broadened.

He sucked harder on one nipple, rubbing the other in slow, deliberate circles, plumping up the tasty globe with slight roughness. Her moan of pleasure was louder this time, experimental. He pulled the material out of the way, grazing his teeth ever so slightly against her pointed nipple.

"*Stephen,*" she said, her fingers lacing through his hair, holding his head captive against her. He took the round areola into his mouth, sucking harder, and she writhed against him, her breathing coming fast and sharp.

He moved his head back, despite her urging. "We're going to take this slow," he said to her, kissing her breastbone, her ribcage, her navel. The shapely mound of Venus, bumping slightly over her pubic bone. He licked her belly button, causing her to laugh in surprise.

Then he lavished attention over her legs, stroking her thighs, kissing the sensitive skin at the back of her knees, the curve of her calves, the shapely arch of her petite foot.

"You touch me like I'm something precious," she said slowly, with wonder in her voice.

"More than you know," he said.

"I'll bet you say that to all the girls," she said, with a nervous, unsure laugh.

He stopped in his ministrations, stretching out alongside her and framing her face with his hands. "I've never said anything like this before in my life," he said. "Not even with the girl I thought I was in love with. I can't even believe what you bring out in me."

She kissed him, emotion drenching the action. He closed his eyes, feeling as if his chest were being squeezed in a vise. He'd never felt like this before. He didn't know that sex could be like this. He felt jolted, wrung out—and eager for more.

He reached down, pushing aside the material of her panties and pressing in slowly with his fingertips. She was already drenched with arousal, ready for him. His cock responded with some moisture of his own, and he felt the familiar compulsion, the almost mind-numbing desire to slide his cock into her, feeling her welcoming warmth enveloping him.

Not yet, he counseled himself. He stroked her breasts, cupping their fullness with his hands, then returned to his kissing exploration, smoothing his lips over the gentle flair of her hips. He grinned at her embroidered decoration. "An apple, huh?" he said. "That's unusual."

"Like Eve and Adam," she said, and her eyes were low lidded as she smiled with delightful wickedness. "Temptation. Want a bite of apple, lover?"

He laughed with pure joy, the sense of freedom exhilarating. "Nothing I'd rather taste," he said, letting the heat of his breath wash over her as he slid the panties down her long, beautiful legs. He parted her thighs, then dipped his tongue into her curls, tasting the honeyed rain of her response.

"Oh God, yes," she moaned with increasing volume, her thighs clutching instinctively tighter, brushing against his cheeks. "Stephen . . ."

He nestled deeper, using his fingers to part the lips of her sex, revealing the nubbin of pleasure. Her clit stood erect, a dark red triangle, and he flicked it with his tongue, then grazed it gently with his teeth. She let out a small, surprised shriek of pleasure. He smiled against her, his cock pulsing with need. He continued working her clit with his mouth as his fingers slowly penetrated her. He pushed in first one, then two, then three fingers. He felt the pulsating ridges of her pussy, feeling high inside her for that special spot. Her breathing was hard, frantic, her lips lifting up from the bed, forcing his fingers even deeper inside her.

Then she stopped, pulling back. "Is something wrong?" he asked, his hand stilling but not retreating.

"Wait," she panted. "Wait."

He pulled away slowly, his fingers wet with her juices. "What is it?"

"Something's missing," she said, and he was disappointed when she angled away from him. "I want something more."

"What?" he asked, surprised.

She was blushing—he could see the rosy stain covering every inch of her delectable flesh. "Lydia told me about something to try," she admitted.

She twisted on the bed, nudging him onto his side. Her still-damp pussy was suddenly right in front of his face. Now, however, her mouth was tantalizingly close to his cock. It strained toward her full lips.

She traced his cock head with her tongue, and he almost lost it, simply at the feeling of her moist, hot mouth. She looked at him, curious. Hesitant.

"You sure?" he asked, his voice harsh with restrained need.

She nodded. "I want you to feel what I'm feeling," she said, promise rich in her voice. "I want us to both feel it."

He sighed as her mouth closed around him. She sucked on him, making long pulling strokes with her mouth, scraping ever so delicately along the ridge of his cock head with the edge of her teeth. Her hand cupped his balls, stroking the skin and the buried base of his cock, making him tremble. He groaned, then burrowed between her thighs, sucking on her clit as his fingers reentered her wet, willing slit.

Her cry of pleasure reverberated against the sensitive flesh of his erection. He moved his hips automatically, then forced himself not to thrust forward, letting her set the pace. Her inexperience and exploration only made the experience that much more erotic. He delved into her cunt with his fingers, stroking her, spreading her.

They stayed like that for a long time, pleasuring each other, bringing each other to the brink of ecstasy. Stephen thought he would explode with the sheer sensation overload careening through his system. The salty, sweet taste of her, the feel of her pussy clenching around his fingers, the way her heated little mouth closed around his cock like a miniature version of her cunt, pushed him close to the edge.

She was suddenly groaning loudly, taking him in even deeper. He sucked harder, nipping at her clit as his fingers pressed in. She cried out against his flesh, her thighs wrapping around his head, and she sucked with increasing pressure, stroking his shaft with both her hands. He felt the convulsions of her pussy, drank in the liquid response of her as she came against his hands. He lost his mind as she milked his cock, and his orgasm burst through him. He groaned against her pussy, his hips bucking as she swiveled her cunt against his eager, probing tongue. He could feel her tongue stroking him as he came, drinking every drop of his ejaculation. The delicate, butterfly-light strokes coaxed an echoing release from his body, and his mind went completely blank as he was overwhelmed by the culmination of their act. He kept sucking on her pussy, kissing it, stroking the rim of delicate flesh of her outer labia with slick-wet fingertips, reveling in the sound of her soft sighs and the shudders of her drawn-out release. She nibbled at his cock, her tongue bathing it with gentle, lapping licks.

Finally, after long moments, he rolled away from her, lying on his back, breathing hard. "Wow," he murmured, breathless. "Just . . . wow."

She moved to face him, nestling in the curve of his arm. "It's amazing," she said. "It's seems to get better, every time. Will it always feel this way?"

He kissed her temple, his arm curling around her protectively. "Only one way to find out," he said, holding her tight.

For the first time ever, he was willing to dedicate the rest of his life to the answer.

An hour later, Beth stood in front of the mirror in the motel room's small bathroom. She hadn't looked in a mirror in ten years. She'd caught reflections of herself in calm portions of the stream, but she hadn't looked at herself, really given herself a prolonged study, in ages. She stared at her own face as if looking at a stranger.

Then there was the rest of her body. She took off the bra, staring at her naked form. One breast had a love mark, from where Stephen had kissed with rough, sucking pressure, something that thrilled her. Her neck had one, as well. Her body was pale and flushed, her eyes bright as torches, her hair falling in curling waves, rioting down her back.

Stephen stood in the doorway, his arms crossed. "You look

amazing," he said, his green eyes glowing like banked fires. His smile was slow and sensuous.

She turned. His naked body was a sight she was more accustomed to than looking at her own, but she never tired of it. He looked like he was chiseled out of marble, hard and magnificent. His cock was hard again, she thought with a delicious shiver of anticipation. "Just seeing you turns me on," she admitted, reaching for him, ready to go back to the king-sized bed and indulge in another round of high-energy sex.

"Have you ever wondered what we look like when we're together?" he said instead, surprising her.

She tilted her head. Then she turned, catching her puzzled expression in the mirror, and understood. "I never thought about it," she said, with growing curiosity.

He stepped behind her, nudging her hair away from her neck, kissing her just below her earlobe. She watched as his lips pressed down her neck, across her shoulder. It was thrilling in an entirely new way. She watched as his hand reached forward to cup her breast, his thumb stroking across the nipple. She watched as the dusky nipple pointed with excitement, the sensation magnified by the fact that she was studying the whole thing closely, watching herself as if she were a stranger. She felt his erection, nudging her in the small of her back. She sighed, rubbing against him, getting up on her tip toes. She felt the heat of him, stroking the cleft of her buttocks. She saw the expression of intense hunger blossoming on her face, watched her hands clench the ridge of the countertop as she arched her back, begging him silently to enter her.

He lowered himself, angling his cock at the entrance of her

pussy, and she saw the ripple of muscles cascade through his body even as she felt the hard length of his erection slowly slide into her wet, tight pussy. She gasped, backing against him, her head thrown back in ecstasy as he slowly entered and withdrew, entered and withdrew.

"You're a little too small for this," he said, pulling out completely, and she made a sound of disappointment. "Wait, wait. Let's try something."

He turned her, and then angled her so she could still see over her shoulder. He propped one of her feet up on the countertop. She could see the dark spear of his cock, standing at attention. She could also see the flash of pink of her cunt, spread wide by her position. Her pulse spiked. She remained riveted to the mirror as she watched her hand reach out, stroking his cock, damp from her arousal.

She looked up to find Stephen staring also, his face dark with desire. "Keep watching," he said, and she saw his large hand wrap around his cock, positioning it between her folds. She watched as the thick head nuzzled her pussy, pushing its way in, his shaft disappearing within her dark curls. He pulled away, then slid back in, using deliberate motions. His hips flexed and moved, and his thumb reached between them, flicking at her tight, hard clit.

She arched her hips, moaning, fingering her breast with one hand as she held on to Stephen for dear life with her other hand. Watching his cock working her pussy in the mirror was indescribable.

He started moving incrementally faster, his breathing going harsh and ragged. She was gasping, moaning, her hips bucking against his hammering penis, watching as they ground against each other, his cock buried up to his hips in her eager cunt.

"I love watching you fuck me," she said, clutching his shoulders, lifting herself so he could have deeper access. "I love the feel of your cock, deep inside my pussy."

"You're so hot," he panted, his hips picking up speed and momentum. She twisted against him, the hard ridge of his cock swiveling against her taut muscles. She cried out at the pleasure, her thighs holding him tight. "You feel so fucking incredible. I want to bury myself in you every day. Every hour. I can't get enough of you."

"Please," she whimpered, in a frenzy. "Please. Make me come, Stephen."

He thrust, high and hard, hitting her G-spot like an archer, and she screamed, the sound of pleasure rippling from her throat in a high vibrato. She slammed against him, her hips working like pistons as she ground against his cock, the aftershocks spiraling through her from her pussy to her heart to her extremities. Afterward, she collapsed against him, breathing heavily.

He was still hard, and sweat beaded his forehead. "I love to feel you come," he said, holding still as she recovered. "I love feeling your pussy clench around me."

"Stephen," she breathed, kissing him hard, and he kissed her back. Then he started to press into her again, slowly at first, with growing speed.

"Beth," he moaned, going deep inside her, his hands clutching at her hips. "Beth, baby, I'm close."

She wrapped her legs around his waist, arching back, her nipples facing him. She tilted her head back, watching as he suckled first one breast, then the other, his hips never slowing in their relentless pace.

She watched herself pinch her nipples, gasping with growing pleasure. She looked down, seeing his cock directly as it disappeared between her thighs. Then she looked up, meeting his eyes.

"I love you," she whispered. "I'll always love you."

He stopped, then leaned forward, kissing her deeply, his tongue twining with hers.

The second orgasm surprised her, but it completed what she was feeling, and she cried out in his mouth, holding onto him.

He moved with renewed strength, slamming into her, her orgasm milking his cock as she moaned loudly, her breathing shallow, her fingers clawing at his back. "Stephen," she moaned. "Oh, Stephen . . . I want you to come inside of me. I want to feel you spurt all hot and liquid in my pussy. . . ."

"I love you," he groaned, his hips bucking against her, his cock pressing deep inside her. "Baby, you make me so hot, I'm gonna come . . ."

"Yes," she cried, her fingers twining in his hair as her body was wrenched with yet another wave of orgasm. *"Yes! Yes! Yes!"*

He shouted as his release shot through him, and she felt all his muscles bunch in his body, the tension turning him into a stone statue as he shuddered through his orgasm. She felt the hot spasm of come shoot inside her, and she clenched around him, the rippling waves of her own orgasm still shaking her to her core.

He fell against her, his head resting on her shoulder. They

stayed that way for a long time, her legs and arms wrapped around him, their heartbeats pounding in synchronization as they came down from their sexual high.

He withdrew, letting out a shaky laugh. "Holy shit," he breathed. "You almost made me pass out, woman."

She laughed, too, delight warring with weariness. "It's the mirror," she said, both embarrassed and fascinated. "I had no idea it could be so arousing."

He smiled. "I'll go out and buy a big mirror for over the bed," he said.

She shivered. She'd remembered people talking about putting a mirror over the bed, but she'd always thought it a bit ridiculous, some sort of banal cliché. Now, the thought excited her.

"What else?" she breathed.

He looked at her. "What else? What else do you want?"

"Everything," she said, reaching for him. "I want to try anything and everything. As long as it's with you."

"As long as it's with me," he murmured back, kissing her, "I approve wholeheartedly. And we will try everything, I promise."

She laughed again. "I don't even know what everything is," she admitted.

"Oh, you know," he said, his tone light even as his eyes lit with sexual speculation. "Food, toys, bondage . . ."

Her eyes widened, and the smile faded from her face.

He laughed, stroking her cheek. "Don't worry. We won't do anything you don't like. Hell, just missionary style is hotter with you than the kinkiest sex I've ever had."

She frowned. "Does it . . . what does all that do?"

He shrugged. "It just makes things different," he said. "Hotter, sometimes. It depends on what you like."

"I want to try whatever you think will make us both feel good," she said, stroking him.

"We've got plenty of time," he said, kissing her.

She smiled, feeling impatient. The freedom she felt—the safety—was intoxicating. And just as arousing, if not more so, than the mirror.

"What else can we do tonight?"

He laughed. "Shower first. Then dinner." His eyes gleamed. "Then . . . we'll see how it goes."

Beth woke to the unfamiliar sensation of a man's arm circling her protectively. She stiffened. Then, slowly, she took a deep breath. Stephen's scent, and the scent of their lovemaking, filled her nostrils.

She was out of the Compound. That fact alone brought a flurry of conflicting emotions: apprehension, excitement . . . fear. But she wasn't alone. She had Stephen, and knowing that created no confusion.

For the first time in a long time, she felt safe, and loved.

She nestled her backside against him, feeling his erection nuzzling against her buttocks, and she smiled.

"Good morning," he mumbled, nipping at her earlobe with his teeth.

She laughed, tilting her head to give him better access. He pressed kisses against her throat, and on the sensitive point just behind her ear. She shivered against him, getting wet automatically. "I feel like I'm still dreaming."

"You're not sore?" he asked, reaching down and rubbing

her pussy with his fingertips. The pressure was delicious, and she parted her thighs, arching her back. "We were pretty busy last night."

"I'm making up for lost time," she said, as he stroked his penis between her thighs, teasing the entrance of her sex. "I can't get enough of you."

He put the head of his penis inside her, caressing the delicate, sensitive rim of flesh at the opening of her pussy. She reared back against him, forcing him deeper inside her. He growled, nudging her onto her knees. She turned willingly, and he withdrew until he was only fractionally inside her, then he plunged into her with one smooth motion. She gasped, then cried out, relishing the freedom: she no longer had to be quiet, keep hidden.

He started to move, slowly, surely, gliding in and out of her in long, steady thrusts. She arched her back, bucking against him, swiveling her hips to bring maximum friction to their lovemaking. "Stephen," she chanted. "Oh, Stephen . . ."

He reached in front of her, stroking her clit with his thumb as his hips continued his sensual onslaught, penetrating her deeply. The sensation was more than she could bear. She screamed in pleasure as she came, and he kept moving relentlessly, causing the orgasm to draw out in rippling, continuous aftershocks.

She collapsed forward on the bed, feeling delightfully wrung out. He nudged her to turn over, then entered her again, facing her. She smiled up at him.

"I love you," he whispered, kissing her. Then he started to move again, more gently this time, his cock moving at a slow-dance tempo, burying himself inside her, his balls slapping gently against her buttocks. She wrapped her legs around his, holding him closer to her, and he kissed her breasts as he stroked inside her, his shaft rubbing against her clit.

She felt the building pressure, and she gasped, kneading his back with her hands. He increased his rhythm, and she could tell from his breathing that he was close.

"I love you, Stephen," she said, then cried out as the orgasm overtook her. He groaned against her shoulder, his hips jerking against her, the friction triggering another orgasm. She felt the hot spurt of his come, and she wrapped her legs around his waist, wanting him deep inside her, as deep as she could get him. He groaned again, bucking against her, his cock shivering against her contracting pussy. Her whole body felt like it was on fire with pleasure, a shimmering pulse of unbelievable erotic sensation.

After long moments, he finally rolled off of her, and they both lay there, spent.

"If we keep this up," Stephen said ruefully, "I'm going to spend the rest of the day sleeping."

"That's not so bad a thing," she said, yawning, stretching out.

He laughed. "We've got to be on the move soon, Beth."

She bit her lip. "I told the delivery woman I'd pay her for smuggling me out," she said.

"I don't like this," he said, propping himself up on one elbow. "It would've been better for you to get an address or something, send her money. I don't like being this close to the Compound. They're going to come looking for you."

"There are plenty of other motels," she assured him,

even as a nervous tremor rippled through her. "And they won't think that I stayed. Besides . . . she helped me, and I promised."

He stared into her eyes, studying her, then nodded. "All right," he said. "We'll stay, pay her, then get out of here. I figure it'll take us about four hours to get home."

"Home?" she asked. She wrapped the sheet around herself, facing him. "Where are we going?"

"New York." He kept his words casual, but she could tell he was trying to gauge her reaction. "My apartment. If you don't mind."

She bit her lip. She'd been trying to ignore the worries that were beginning to gnaw at her. She had already changed her name, sort of. She no longer had the fake passport that she'd bribed a palace servant to get her, the one saying she was Beth Anderson, or something. It'd been years since she'd seen it, and couldn't even remember the fake last name. As a Penitent, she had never needed any sort of identification: she'd never had any interaction with the outside world. She'd never gotten a driver's license, never gotten a checking account, never paid taxes. As far as the system was concerned, she didn't exist.

Which was how she'd like to keep it.

But what will I do? Depend on Stephen for everything? Stay hidden for the rest of my life?

She frowned. That's exactly what she had done as a Penitent. She'd depended on them completely, and lived her life at their whim. She was starting to see that, while she'd thought she was safe, she wasn't free.

Now that she knew what freedom felt like, she didn't think she wanted to go back to dependence. Not even depending on someone she loved.

"It'll be okay," Stephen said, responding to worry he must have seen in her face. "Trust me."

"I do," she replied automatically. "Trust you, I mean."

He smiled. "I love you. And I'll take care of you."

She pulled away from his caressing fingertips. "I can take care of myself," she said, although her voice was unsteady.

"I know you can," he agreed. "But for a while, I want you to know that you don't have to."

"All right." She felt uncomfortable. "I'll take care of you, too, then."

"I'm looking forward to that," he said, leering playfully. Then he got out of bed, giving her an eyeful of his fine masculine physique. *I'm looking forward to it, too*, she thought, some of the grim mood shaking off. "You hungry?" he asked.

"Ravenous," she replied, realizing it was true—although, as usual, she was just as hungry for him as she was for food. Still, with all their physical exertion, she desperately needed to refuel.

"Tell you what. They don't have much in the way of room service around here, but there's a diner around the corner. I'll go get us some breakfast and bring it back, okay?"

She nodded, then frowned. "I need to ask another favor."

He paused, his shirt half over his head. "Anything."

"Is there a clothing store nearby?" She looked at her Penitent dress, balled up on the floor. "My old clothes draw too much attention."

"Good point," he agreed. "I'll go grab you some new clothes."

"I don't even know what my size is," she said, standing up and turning.

His gaze roamed over her body, like a physical touch. She tingled everywhere he looked.

"I think I know your body well enough to find something that would fit you." A smile warmed his voice, but his eyes blazed with intensity.

She almost reached for him. "You'd better go," she said softly, "or I might never let you leave."

He looked torn. Then he sighed, kissing her hard. "I'll be back soon," he promised, then left.

She hugged herself for a moment. *He is wonderful.*

After a few minutes, she tidied up the room, more out of habit and nervous energy than anything. She put her old clothes in a bag. She didn't want to wear any of it—not even the large, unsightly white cotton underwear. Still, sitting around naked felt way too decadent, especially without Stephen there to make it seem natural.

She slipped into the apple-decorated lingerie, then did an experimental stroll in front of the bathroom mirror, shivering at the memory of their encounter in front of it, just last night. With her black hair rumpled and wavy, her cheeks pink with excitement, and her blue eyes bright, she looked different than she could ever remember herself looking before. She looked confident. Alluring. She tried a mock pout, her full lips bowing coyly, then she laughed at herself for her absurdity.

It was the laugh that jogged her memory, and the smile froze on her face.

It was as if her mother was staring back at her from the mirror.

She traced the contour of her face in the glass with her fingertip. Was that what her stepmother had always seen in her? And hated?

Was that why her father had kept away from her until his own untimely death?

She closed her eyes. It wasn't her fault. Just as it wasn't her fault that her stepmother hated her for that resemblance. Beth had been a walking reminder that the former Queen had been both beautiful and talented, and that the King would love and mourn his dead wife forever, despite his re-marriage.

She'd been young and terrified when she'd run away to the forest, to the seven Founders who had promised her safety and anonymity, so long as she cleaned their house, cooked their food, and stayed a pure and virtuous maiden, following their orders.

She opened her eyes, staring at her face.

She wasn't young and terrified anymore. She was through with running away.

There was a banging on the door.

Her breath caught in her throat. It obviously wasn't Stephen. Whoever it was, he meant business. This was no knock for entry: it was the heavy thumb of someone trying to break in. The motel was cheap enough that security doors weren't a high priority.

She looked around frantically. The window in the bathroom was tiny, too small to crawl out of, no doubt to prevent people from slipping out without paying their bills. The only window was in the room itself, by the door. It would not help her escape.

She had to hide. Again, the motel room provided little assistance. They would look in the obvious places: the closet, underneath the bed. Where could she hide that would not be obvious?

She glanced at the cabinet in the bathroom, beneath the sink. It was empty, and tiny, but large enough for a small person. She contorted herself hastily, closing the door just as the front door of the room smashed in.

"Beth!"

It was Founder Amos's voice. She'd recognize it anywhere. The naked sound of fury in his tone sent spikes of ice through her heart. He sounded downright murderous.

"She's not here." This from Founder Timothy, sounding his usual sour self. "Breaking down the door is attracting too much attention, Robert! Are you insane?"

"She hasn't gone," Founder Robert countered stubbornly. "I know it. She's still here. The man said they had not checked out yet."

"Perhaps they simply ran," Timothy said.

"She's still here."

This came from a woman. Beth held her breath. The voice held a slight rasp, but otherwise was low and regal, and painfully familiar.

The Queen!

How? How had she found Beth, after all this time?

"Why should we believe you?" Founder Robert's voice

was derisive. "You're only a delivery woman. And it's your fault that she's off the Compound in the first place! You smuggled her out!"

Smuggled me out? Beth's mind raced as she tried to process what she had just heard.

The horribly deformed delivery woman . . . was her stepmother?

How was that possible?

"I wasn't wrong about Lydia and those others," her stepmother said smugly. "Besides, Founder Amos didn't believe that she'd actually leave. I knew this was the only way to convince him." There was an undertone of evil satisfaction in her voice. "And convince him to punish her accordingly."

"That's quite enough," Founder Amos said. "I'll believe it when I . . ."

Beth heard the door slam open. "Beth!"

It was Stephen. Her heart slammed in her chest, and she bit her lip to keep from yelling.

She heard sounds of a scuffle. Her blood froze as the sounds turned muffled, and Stephen was silenced.

"Believe me now?" Her stepmother's voice was triumphant. "Where did you put her then, handsome? Where is our little girl?"

"She's not here?" Stephen sounded relieved. "Then you haven't got her. She made it out."

"She won't get far," Founder Robert promised.

"You." Founder Amos sounded furious. "You took her away from me. From *us*. You corrupted her with your lust!"

"You were keeping her trapped in that life of yours," Stephen said. "If she's free now, it was all worth it."

He loved her that much. She swallowed hard.

"If we can't find her," Amos said, "your punishment will be severe. Even by our measures. Timothy, Robert . . . take him."

Beth felt a scream building in her chest. She could live if she just stayed hidden. If she ran away. But she was condemning the man she loved to death.

I'm not going to run anymore.

She wrenched herself out of the cupboard. Opening the bathroom door, she stepped out, not caring about her appearance. She saw the door, hanging from its hinges, propped against the doorframe. Stephen was being held by Robert and Timothy. Amos was arguing with the delivery woman, her stepmother.

"I'm here," she said.

The Founders stared at her, slack jawed. Her stepmother stared at her as well, her twisted face a grotesque mask of fury and disbelief.

"Beth," Founder Amos said, his vocal cords obviously strained to near breaking with disbelief and fury. "What has he done to you?"

"Nothing I didn't want him to do," she answered. "I wanted him. This was *my* choice. Do whatever you want to me, but leave him alone."

"No!" Stephen struggled, and Robert hit him hard in the stomach. He fell to his knees.

Amos took a step closer to her. She could smell his breath, tinged with pipe tobacco. "You could have been safe with me," he whispered.

She stood her ground, her chin up. "But I wouldn't have

been happy," she said. "Please. It's me you're angry at. Let him go."

He sighed, his gaze fixating on the apple on her panties. She felt unclean. "You will learn that safety is much preferable," he answered slowly. "I hope it was worth it. I hope that your *happiness* was worth dying for."

"Timothy," he said, "take her."

Timothy held a handkerchief to Stephen's face briefly, then let him go, leaving Stephen shaking his head and swaying dizzily on his knees. Then Timothy grabbed her arm. She struggled, but he pinned her wrist painfully behind her back.

"And Robert," Amos said, his voice full of distaste, "dispose of him. Painfully."

Beth realized her action had been for nothing. "No!" she screamed, but the handkerchief was in front of her face now, and within moments, her vision grayed to black, and she fell.

Chapter Fourteen

"What . . . are you going to do . . . to Beth?" Stephen asked, as best he could.

Robert had taken him from the motel in the back of his SUV, and now they were in a forest—not on the Compound. Someplace else. The perfect place to leave a body, Stephen realized. He closed his eyes for a second. The combination of the ether or whatever Timothy had nailed him with, and Robert's blows to his head, were making him dizzy, so closing his eyes didn't really help matters. He focused on Robert's voice, trying to triangulate the man's position by sound.

Robert's fist came flying out of the darkness, hitting Stephen hard and sending him sprawling against tree roots. *So much for triangulation.*

He needed to come up with a new plan, and fast.

"It's amazing how stupid men become," Founder Robert

marveled, circling Stephen's crumbled form, "just by look-ing at that little whore's face."

"Don't call her a whore," Stephen snarled, trying hard to focus, his fists flailing out.

Robert dropped him neatly with a quick right jab. "I'll call her whatever I want," he replied, almost amused. "We never should have taken her in. I told Amos that from the begin-ning. But the man wanted her. 'She'll strengthen our resolve. She'll test our faith. She shouldn't be further punished for a flaw she never chose.' What rubbish!"

Robert kicked Stephen hard in the stomach, knocking the wind out of him. He landed hard at the base of an oak.

The man was unleashing a lot of fury here, a small, quiet, rational part of Stephen's brain pointed out, as he struggled to breathe. Robert could've merely killed Stephen by now, but he obviously wanted to beat some punishment into Stephen first, rather than give the easy out of a painless death. He was emo-tional, not rational. Maybe he could be goaded into making a mistake.

Unfortunately, for an older guy, Robert was built like a tank. He also had years of repression and craziness adding to his sheer physical strength. Stephen gasped as he slowly regained oxygen. Goading this guy might not be the wisest course of action.

So what to do?

"I guess Amos is pretty pissed," Stephen said slowly. "Beth is obviously a favorite of his."

"Fool," Robert spat out.

"So . . . maybe Amos is just going to keep her chained up for his own amusement." The thought sickened Stephen.

"How do you Founders feel about that? About Amos having his own rules? He's obviously the guy in charge. You guys are just hired help."

Stephen was trying to divert Robert's fury. To his chagrin, Robert only laughed.

"Even Amos wouldn't touch her now, and he knows the consequences. We've got something special planned for the little slut." The note of gleeful anticipation in the older man's voice was sickening.

"What are you going to do?" Stephen asked, getting to his feet.

Robert aimed another vicious kick at him, sending him sprawling. Stephen picked himself up slowly, advancing.

"You outsiders think you're better than us," Robert said. "You think that your lack of morals somehow makes you more cosmopolitan. You think we're insane for living principled lives."

"You are fucking insane," Stephen spat out, raising his fists. The last hints of the drug finally dissipated, leaving him in pain—and fueled with rage of his own. "You think that you're gods, and all those people are your own private ant farm. You and Amos and the rest of them. You're just a bunch of freaks!"

Robert's face turned purple. "We are the Founders," he intoned, and he sounded like he really believed it . . . that he was some sort of a god. "We are the law."

"You are a bunch of psychotic assholes," Stephen said. "And if anything happens to Beth, I'll kill you."

"You're going to die right here," Robert taunted. "As for the whore, she'll regret the day she ever seduced you." Robert sounded sickened—and vaguely excited. "Vanity, lust. Everyone in the Compound will know the true ugliness of her and her sex when we banish her."

Everything went still inside Stephen's head.

"What are you going to do?" he asked, his voice seemingly disembodied as the world focused to a point.

"The Penitents have lost their way," Robert said, producing a knife and stepping toward Stephen. "She will serve as a reminder for those who do not follow the true path."

"*What are you going to do?*" Stephen repeated, not retreating. The knife gleamed just a foot away.

"She wants to be seen," Robert said. "We're going to make sure that everyone sees her. They'll watch her suffer. Then, they'll watch her die."

The man's cavalier, enthusiastic attitude set something off in Stephen, something he didn't even know he could feel. He was through planning, scheming, trying to figure out a way around this guy.

This man was going to kill Beth. That was all he needed to know.

Robert lunged at him with the knife, and Stephen dodged, feeling the blade cut his shoulder deeply with a glancing blow. With a loud, anger-filled bellow, Stephen went for Robert, tackling him, slamming him against the tree. He slammed the man's head against the trunk, hard. Robert fell, dazed. Stephen started beating him, his fists connecting heavily, cracking and bleeding from the repeated connection with Robert's hard jaw. He heard something break, but kept on hitting.

With a gurgling cry of surprise, Robert fell to the ground,

his eyes glazed. Stephen wrestled the knife out of Robert's hand. For a second, he thought about slicing Robert's throat—the satisfaction he would get from killing the man who would murder the woman he loved.

But he couldn't. He wasn't crazy. And Beth was still alive.

He tossed the knife to one side, then kicked Robert. Robert fell like a downed tree, unconscious. Stephen left him there, limping slightly as he hurried to Robert's SUV. The man didn't have a cell phone. He had to get to the police. His arm hurt, but he ignored it.

He drove down the road, finding a convenience store. He used the pay phone to call Lieutenant Grady.

"They're going to kill her," he said, without preamble.

"Kill who?"

"Beth," Stephen said.

"Son, I told you . . ."

"They're going to kill her on the premises," Stephen said. "In front of witnesses. I don't know how, but they've already drugged me and stabbed me, and I know that they're going to do worse—"

"They stabbed you?" Now Grady perked up. "Damn! Now we've got 'em. You sit tight, I'll have a black-and-white out to get you and then we'll—"

"There's no time!" Stephen spat out. "They're going to kill her!"

"Don't go in there," Grady warned. "You've done your part, and now it's our turn. Just stay put."

"No," Stephen said. Fast or not, the police would take too much time to mobilize. Robert made it sound like the punishment would be fast. Beth could be dead by the time they arrived.

"Stephen, don't do anything stupid . . ."

"I'll meet you there," he said, then hung up and got in the SUV.

He sped down the highway toward the Compound.

"Let this be a lesson to all of you!"

It was early afternoon, and the sun was sweltering, but she felt no warmth or comfort. The Commons was filled with people, women to one side, men to the other. There were torches lit, ones that were normally reserved for seasonal celebrations or night sermons.

Beth shivered. She was still wearing the bright red lingerie with the apple, her hair falling to her waist. Everyone was staring at her, and she squirmed at their scrutiny. She would have been embarrassed if she weren't so painfully aware of the fact that they were going to hurt her, or worse.

They were making this a spectacle, she realized. Lydia, Henry, and Camille's banishment was going to seem like a small, simple gesture by comparison.

"For years, we have tried to forgive Goodmaid Beth for the temptation of her face," Founder Amos intoned. "But she has turned her back on our good nature, giving in to the most base and scandalous of transgressions. She left the Compound. She has seduced a Goodman into temptation. She has given herself over to *lust*."

The crowd was being lashed by his words, wincing with each theatric outburst. They were silent, but Beth could still feel the bloodlust whipping through them, worse than with

Lydia, worse than she'd ever experienced. They were held in thrall.

Her eyes picked out Goodmaid Amelia, Goodman Joshua. *I can't believe they'd hurt me.*

But from the sounds of it, the Founders had a lot more than mere pain in mind.

In the midst of it all, her stepmother stood, now wearing one of the plain dresses of a Penitent. Her face was still grotesque, a physical echo of the twistedness of her mental state. As Founder Amos continued his diatribe, her stepmother sidled up to where Beth was chained.

"I've lived for this day," her stepmother murmured, her voice for Beth's ears alone. "I knew you were still alive. I knew I'd find you."

Beth looked at the Queen, her voice strangely detached.

"What happened to your face?"

Her stepmother blanched, taken aback. "Nothing that can't be reversed," she snapped. "I was just about to see Dr. Weissen to correct the damage he'd done, when one of my private detectives stumbled across a servant who used to work in the palace. It appears he'd come across a lot of money and had moved off the island, but now, broke and drunken, he told stories of how you weren't dead." She smiled, and it pulled her mouth up on one side in a cruel slash. "I made sure he was brought back to Iko, and my guards forced him to tell me exactly what he did to help you. It took longer than I thought, but I finally discovered the rock you crawled under."

Beth didn't say anything.

"I decided I'd put off the surgery until after I dealt with

you," her stepmother finished. "I knew you'd recognize me otherwise. And once I got here, I realized that these men would do the job for me. I don't even have to get my hands dirty. I just had to make sure that you did just what I needed you to do to get you punished."

Beth's eyes widened. The chocolate. The lingerie. The condoms. Every "temptation" the delivery woman had offered . . . all poisonous gifts, meant to get her exactly where she was now.

"And you never recognized me," her stepmother said triumphantly.

"Dr. Weissen," Beth murmured. He was the Queen's favored plastic surgeon. She'd been going to him since before she was wed. "He did this to you? You mean, you've had so much plastic surgery done that this is what happened to you."

Her stepmother's eyes narrowed, and her face mottled with anger.

"You've always wanted to be beautiful, and young," Beth noted, almost clinically. "You've got a surgery addiction. You've had so much work done that you're trying desperately to stop what's left of your face from disintegrating completely."

"You smug little bitch!" her stepmother hissed. And Beth knew immediately that she was right.

"I will say this, though," Beth continued calmly. "You're a better actress than I ever gave you credit for."

Her stepmother took a step toward her, arm raised to strike. Founder Timothy stopped her before the blow fell.

"She's not to be marked, woman," he said sternly.

Her stepmother was livid. "How dare you! Do you know who I am?"

"I don't care," he replied. "Be still, or you'll be next. Founder Amos is determined, and his anger . . ." He let the words peter out, even as a vicious gleam lit up his expression.

The Queen fell silent. "I will enjoy watching you die," she finally said, then stepped away from Beth.

Beth took a deep breath. She'd stood up to her stepmother.

Too bad it had taken her this long—and that it had to end this way.

"Bring her forward," Founder Amos said, beckoning to Timothy.

Timothy unchained her from the post, dragging her up and shoving her at Amos's feet. She whimpered slightly as her knees hit the planking of the dais.

"You were the most beautiful woman I'd ever seen," Founder Amos whispered, reaching out and almost touching a lock of her hair that had fallen in front of her eyes. Then he flinched, pulling his hand back as though she held something communicable. For all she knew, perhaps she did. Perhaps lust was something that, once experienced, might spread by sheer proximity.

"You knew your beauty was a temptation. You knew that sex was a danger—a pitfall that all of us have vowed to turn our back on. We are not animals, bound to our basest urges!"

She forced herself to stand. "Having sex with Stephen was not base," she said clearly, her voice carrying. "It was—and is—love. I shared my body with him because I fell in love with him, and it was worth whatever it is you're going to do to me."

She didn't know what disappointed him more: that she'd given up her innocence or that she was now defying him in front of the entire Penitent congregation. He looked stunned, mortified. Furious.

"You tempted him, with your . . . with *this*," he said, gesturing to her near naked body. "You seduced him. You used your beauty as a weapon, and the only thing that you served was your vanity!"

He grabbed her wrist, painfully, yanking her to her feet. "Is this what you want, then? To be admired? To be kept beautiful, seductive, forever?"

He did not wait for her response.

"Bring forth the box!"

The box? She wondered if she would be buried alive. She craned her neck, trying to see, but he forced her back to her knees.

Four of the Founders carried a large glass box. She did not remember ever seeing it before.

"When we started the Penitents, we had one such as you. Beautiful, pristine . . . at least on the surface." Now Founder Amos was talking to the crowd as well as Beth. "She broke our rules. She thought we would ignore her vanity and her wantonness. But she was punished. She *had* to be punished. And we made sure that she understood the price of vanity."

Beth caught a look at the Queen, whose eyes gleamed with triumph.

"You will be placed on display, to be viewed and coveted

by all in the Compound," he said, as they opened the box. "You will be sealed inside your case, until you run out of air. And you'll be buried, just as beautiful as the day you die."

She realized abruptly why the shape of the box was so familiar.

It was a glass coffin . . . and they were about to seal her in.

Chapter Fifteen

Stephen drove full tilt in Robert's SUV, heading toward the Penitent Compound. He didn't see police cars there, which backed his theory: the warrant would take too much time. There were Goodmen guarding the gate. They recognized the SUV, and Stephen prayed that they wouldn't look too closely at the driver.

He wasn't that lucky.

"Where is Founder Robert?" one of the men asked. He wasn't armed—none of them were—but he stood in front of the gate, his arms crossed. "You aren't supposed to be driving his car."

They had to know what was going on.

"Get out of my way," Stephen said.

The man's face was carved from granite. "You're no longer

a Penitent," he said, with a note of challenge. "You do not belong here. Turn around, and you won't get hurt."

"I don't have time for this shit," Stephen said. "I'm going in there, period. You can either watch from the sidelines, or watch from under the tires, pal."

The man stood, taciturn.

Stephen threw the SUV in reverse, revved the engine, then pounded his foot to the floor. The Goodman barely got out of the way before Stephen slammed into the metal gate, the force throwing him forward against the steering wheel. The SUV was sturdy, a true four-wheel-drive off-road special, so it wasn't that damaged.

Stephen threw it in reverse again.

Now the other guards were yelling, those on the inside of the gate running down the dirt road, the ones on the outside staring in disbelief as Stephen rammed the gate a second, then a third time. The gate groaned, then finally toppled, the hinges twisted and torn from their posts.

He plowed forward, the SUV climbing over the metal carnage that was the front gate. He sped past the running guards, heading for the Commons.

Beth worked furiously at the rope that held her hands and feet bound. They had her propped up, like a display case, for all the rest of the Penitents to look. She had screamed as they put her in the box, screamed while Founder Timothy sealed the lid shut. Then she'd stopped screaming as she realized he had, indeed, made the box airtight. She could hear the outside world, muffled due to the thick glass, but it was like being trapped inside her own head. The glass fogged from her nervous, shallow breathing.

Unable to loosen her bonds, she slammed her body against first one side, then the other, of the coffin. The glass was too hard against her bare skin. Every breath she took was more oxygen used, less oxygen to spare, but she kept struggling. She stared out at the crowd. The Goodmaids were staring at her with a mix of disgust and fear, as if somehow, one of them might be in a glass box someday. Some women were jeering, catcalling. She couldn't distinguish voices, but she could read lips.

Die, whore!

She glanced over at the men. Several had picked up the same chant. Others were staring at her, also with fear . . . but underneath, the sharp bite of lust. She pressed her chest against the glass, mouthing a plea: "Help me!"

Several men took a step forward, but none acted.

She threw herself back. The Founders looked grim but determined. Amos stared at only her, his arms crossed, his glasses glinting in the fading light.

She gasped slightly, realizing that the air was starting to run out. Her heart beat frantically, and she rattled inside her glass prison. Slowly, her attempts grew slower, weaker.

The last face she saw was her stepmother's grotesque mask of plastic surgery, smiling triumphantly. Then everything went black.

Stephen knew that the Penitents would be there in full force. They flooded the Commons, surrounding the raised dais. They weren't intentionally stopping him, but their bodies blocked the way. He brought Robert's SUV to a screeching halt. He knew that they were in many ways tacitly responsible for what was happening to Beth, but they were sheep. He couldn't simply run them over with the car to get to her, it wasn't right. He got out and struggled against the crowd. "Let me through!"

"What are you doing?" a Goodman asked. "You left the Penitents! Transgressor!"

Stephen felt hands gripping at his clothes, shoving at him. A few punches landed, and he struggled, swinging out. Then a big, burly man stepped next to him.

"We've got to stop this."

It was Goodman Joshua. Stephen took a deep, grateful breath. Joshua moved forward, helping clear the way.

"She must be punished!" a female voice shrieked.

"But must she be killed?" This from another female.

The place was devolving. The Founders had finally pushed too far, and the resulting act wasn't putting the Penitents in their place: it was tearing the Compound apart. Stephen started shoving his way through the crowd, forcing his way toward the dais. The gray-garbed Penitents eyed him warily, before parting, finally giving him a view of the spectacle they were all witnessing.

He stopped in sheer shock at what he saw.

Beth!

She was wearing the sexy red lingerie that she'd greeted him with on her first night of "freedom" at the motel. The tempting apple still sat just below her equally tempting navel.

Her eyes were closed, her chest still.

His heart caught in his throat, and he started to run.

As he got closer, he noticed the shape of the glass case she was sealed up in. It was shaped like a coffin. He hadn't been gone that long, had he? Apparently Robert had taken him in the opposite direction, eating up time. And it didn't really take that long without air.

She looked almost asleep, her shining black hair tumbling rich and lustrous about her pale shoulders, her arms behind her back, her delicate feet bound with heavy rope.

The Founders lined up in front of the coffin, arms crossed, faces menacing. "You don't belong here," Founder Amos pronounced. "*You* brought her to this."

"You couldn't stand that she was a woman. That she liked sex—with someone else," Stephen yelled. "You wanted to keep her for yourself! She told me!"

The crowd let out a shocked murmur at this.

Stephen's hands bunched into fists, and adrenaline shot through his system. "If I have to take you all on, one at a time or all at once," he said, "I'll do it. *Now get out of my way.*"

He heard a stir behind him, then he heard Joshua's voice. "I'm with Stephen," he said quietly. "This is wrong, no matter what she's done, and we all know it. After what happened with Lydia and the others, I can't stand by and watch gain."

To Stephen's surprise, another voice joined Joshua's. "She was a good girl." This, from the round-faced Good-maid Amelia. She sounded determined, and when Stephen glanced at her, he noticed she was rolling up her sleeves . . . a clear violation of the rules. She was ready to fight.

Founder Amos stepped forward, his face the picture of

fury. "You are the one who deserves to die, along with her," he said, and took a swing at Stephen.

Amos was nowhere near as physically imposing as Robert, although he was even more vicious underneath. He was also slow and clumsy. Stephen dodged the blow, landing a right cross of his own across the man's bearded face. Amos's glasses flew off and he fell to the wooden planking, dazed.

The other Founders leaped into the fray, and Joshua took Stephen's side, fending off the attack. Most of the Founders, control freaks but not physical bullies, fled after a few glancing punches. Timothy lumbered forward, his eyes alight with a crazed high. He grappled with Joshua. Amelia surprised them all by going for his groin, wrenching him hard enough to cause a high-pitched scream of shock. Apparently, all those years doing "women's work" gave her enormous upper body strength. Timothy fell like a shot rhino.

Stephen sprinted for the glass coffin, searching for a way to open it. The lead sealing it was too tight. He shoved it off of its stand, but the glass was thick. It didn't break. She fell against the side, her body limp.

No! She can't die!

Stephen grabbed one of the metal torch holders that flanked the dais. Swinging it, he struck the glass. It barely nicked it. He swung harder, throwing his whole body into it. The glass spider-webbed, and he took one last shot.

Fragments showered over Beth's still body. Using the torch holder as a makeshift crowbar, he pried the lid off, picking her up. She was dead weight in his arms. He stretched her out, feeling at her neck and wrist.

He couldn't feel a pulse.

He barely registered the wail of sirens, signaling the arrival of the police. There was fighting among the Penitents. Amos was out cold. Joshua and Amelia were trying to establish some sort of order.

Please don't die!

Stephen put his mouth on hers, struggling to remember his CPR, now when it was most important. He blew hard, then pressed against her chest.

Don't leave me!

She couldn't die. Now that he'd found her, he didn't know how he would live if she died.

"Good God," he heard Lieutenant Grady say behind him. "What the hell is all this?"

Stephen counted out measured beats as he pressed against her heart. "Get an ambulance," he barked, then went to give her another breath.

Before his lips touched hers, she started to cough. He propped her up, cradling her in his arms, feeling tears of relief gather at the corners of his eyes.

"Stephen?" She clung to him. "Stephen. You came."

He held her tight. "Don't ever leave me again," he whispered.

"Never," she replied, and held on tight.

"I think this is the end of the Penitents," Lieutenant Grady said solemnly.

Beth was wrapped in a blanket, still shivering from her near miss. The Penitents were all rounded up, like animals, as police questioned them. The Founders were all under arrest, she wasn't sure for what charges. Attempted murder, possibly first-degree murder for Lydia and her lovers. Who knew what else.

"It's over," Stephen said. "The whole thing is finally over."

She nodded, feeling numb.

"You have no identification whatsoever?" Lieutenant Grady asked her.

"No," she said. "They took it when we joined the Penitents."

Which was true enough, she thought.

"Well, maybe your family could help you get new copies," Grady said helpfully. "I'm sure they'd love to hear from you. It must have been years."

She didn't answer. She looked at Stephen, to see him staring at her.

"We'll take care of it," he told her, putting an arm around her shoulders and squeezing, conveying comfort.

She smiled at him, grateful.

Then, suddenly, her eyes narrowed.

Her family . . .

"Where is she?" she asked, standing up, holding the blanket tightly around her.

Grady and Stephen exchanged confused looks. "Where is who?" Stephen asked.

"The . . . the delivery woman," she said. "She was dressed as a Penitent. She . . . her face is deformed, one cheek higher than the other, her nose askew . . ."

Grady frowned. "Let me ask," he said. "Is she important?"

"She worked with the Founders," she said. "She's the one who helped them find me, and Stephen."

Grady went to talk to the other detectives. Stephen waited

until he was gone, then whispered to her, "The delivery woman, huh?"

"It's worse," Beth whispered back. "She's my stepmother."

"The Queen?" Stephen's voice was shocked. "Here?"

But before she could answer, Grady came back, looking puzzled.

"Nobody matching that description is here among the Penitents," he said. "Are you sure she was here?"

Beth looked around frantically, then bit her lip.

The Queen had gone, disappeared in the confusion. Which meant she was still out there . . . waiting.

"So this is where you live," Beth said quietly, studying the place curiously.

Stephen shrugged. "It's a place I sleep," he answered. "Not really what I would call home."

It was opulent, especially when contrasted with the Spartan quarters that Beth had grown accustomed to. It was large, on a high floor with a view over Central Park. The view from the living room could be a postcard. The kitchen was spacious and well-appointed, with stainless steel pots hanging from a rack over a center island. The living room had overstuffed suede couches and a heavy glass coffee table. There were built-in bookcases, ceiling to floor, taking up one wall. A huge, flat television took up the other. She hadn't seen anything like it. It all felt otherworldly and alien to her, and she hugged herself.

He put an arm around her. "How are you holding up?" he asked, tenderness rich in his voice. "You must be exhausted."

She nodded. They'd spent the better part of the night and most of the day at the police station, answering questions. Founder Amos was under arrest, along with the other Founders, for her attempted murder. Apparently, by morning, one of the Founders had confessed, blubbering in fear, trying to cut himself a deal. So they added the deaths of Lydia and her lovers, who apparently were killed and buried in a wooded grove off the interstate. The rest of the Penitents were released. Many of them, bewildered and disappointed by the falling of their prophets, were at a loss.

Beth felt pity for them.

News crews had scented the blood in the water, and they'd swarmed the Penitent camp and the police station, hungry for the salacious story. Beth had avoided having her picture taken, with Stephen's help, but she knew it would just be a matter of time. So now, she was avoiding the press's relentless curiosity, as well as her deformed stepmother's less benign interest.

Don't think about it. You're safe now. For the moment.

"How about a bath?" Stephen asked. "It'll help you unwind."

She nodded again, silently. She walked into his bedroom. He had a huge, opulent master suite: the bathroom had a large marble tub, and his bed was king-sized, but far more luxurious than the bed they'd had at the motel, the covers pulled back to reveal smooth cream-colored sheets beneath a liquid-shiny silver comforter. "No mirrored ceiling?" she asked, her voice shaky.

"I'll call to have one installed next week," he teased, turning the water on in the bath.

She smiled weakly. She wanted to forget everything, but she doubted a bath would help her wash away the memories: the glass case closing, the air slowly disappearing as she slammed her shoulders against the slick surface . . .

Don't think about it!

Stephen walked behind her, enfolding her in his arms. "It's going to take some time," he murmured, "but I'll do whatever you need to help you get through it."

She leaned back, smiling as he nuzzled the top of her head with the bottom of his chin. Knowing that he cared, that he loved her, was enough to take the edge off. "Better now," she said, turning and hugging him tightly. "Thank you. For this, for everything. For saving my life."

He kissed her gently. "I don't know what kind of life I'd have, if you weren't here," he replied, his voice raw with emotion. "I don't ever want to find out."

She kissed him back, melting into him. His fingers flexed at her waist, and she felt his cock, growing stiff between them. She felt her own hunger begin to rise, drowning out her fear.

He pulled away. "I'm sorry," he said. "Your bath's going to turn cold. I want to make sure you're comfortable."

Implying that sex might make her somehow uncomfortable. Suddenly, she realized it might be just the answer she was looking for. When he started to step back, she followed him, taking off her clothes. "Maybe you could take a bath with me," she said, her voice full of invitation. She stroked her breast.

He seemed riveted by her action, and he nodded. "Maybe I could."

He took off his clothes. His body was glorious, as always, she realized, tracing her fingertips over the chiseled muscles of his torso. He winced as she rubbed over the bruises that Founder Robert had given him. "You're hurt," she said, feeling guilty and selfish.

"Not too hurt for you," he said, his eyes gleaming like a sorcerer's. "The day I'm too hurt to make love to you is the day I'm dead."

She smiled, stroking her hand lower to where his cock stuck out, proud and hard, filling her hand and then some. He groaned lightly, pushing forward, and she saw the bead of glistening moisture at the tip of his penis. She leaned down, lapping at it with her tongue, and his groan turned louder.

"I'm never going to get enough of you," he said, his fingers tangling through her hair.

She knew exactly how he felt.

The tub was full of bubbles, scented a warm and exotic jasmine. She held his hand as she stepped in slowly. "Perfect," she sighed, as the hot water caressed her skin. She parted her legs, putting a foot on either side of the tub. "Come on in."

He smiled at her double entendre, placing himself between her thighs.

For a moment, they just held each other in the heated comfort of the bath, kissing slowly, their bodies slippery from the soap and the water. They were both bruised and beaten and tired, but holding each other was like a balm for both body and soul. Beth held him like a talisman, her protection against the hurts of the world. She kissed his chiseled jaw, nibbled at his earlobe. Her full breasts slid across his wet chest. He caressed them, cupping them in his palms, stroking the sides with his work-roughened fingertips. She leaned her head back against the cool marble, and she felt his cock brushing against her curls.

"I love you," he whispered, reaching into the water. His fingertips pierced the nest of curls between her thighs, searching for and finding her clit. He stroked her with supreme gentleness, and she gasped softly. He continued his gentle exploration, staring into her low-lidded eyes, and she felt the precursors of climax start to build. When the orgasm struck, she let it roll over her, crying out his name, letting herself go limp and liquid beneath him.

He positioned his cock at her opening, sliding inside her with a slow, easy motion. Once inside, he stilled, embracing her. They stayed like that, in each others' arms, their bodies joined beneath the water, for long moments, cherishing the feel of each other. Gaining reassurance.

"I didn't know what my life could be until I met you," she breathed, kissing his neck. "I didn't know I could love anyone this much."

He leaned down, sucking on first one breast, then the other. Her body stirred to life, even after the last powerful orgasm. She felt like he was simply melding with her, his pleasure bleeding into her own. They moved like dancers, slow grace and fluid passion. He stroked inside her cunt with his cock, filling her, caressing her with his blunt cock head. She wrapped her legs around his, and wrapped her arms around his powerful shoulders as he slowly penetrated her, then withdrew, only to press forward again. Warm water lapped at the sides of the bath, sounding like the sea lapping at white sand beaches.

Like Iko, she thought dreamily, a fleeting memory of her childhood home flashing across her mind. Then she shut her eyes, focusing on the pleasure he was giving her, the sense of love and closeness unlike anything she'd ever felt.

He closed his eyes. His face was gorgeous, just as powerfully attractive to her now as the first moment she'd seen him, in the Dining Hall at the Compound. She felt her pussy clench around him, and she sighed his name, matching him thrust for thrust.

"I couldn't bear it if anything happened to you," he whispered, his forehead resting against hers as his hips continued to move. "I want to be with you forever. I want you to stay with me."

"I'll stay with you," she promised. "I love you."

"I love you," he murmured against her lips. His tempo picked up, and they clung to each other, making love as if it were the last time.

Or the first.

"Say my name," she breathed against his hot flesh as the orgasm began to crescendo.

"Beth," he gasped. "Oh God, Beth."

"No," she said, her hips rising to meet his, her eyes shut tight. "Say my real name."

She felt the hesitation, his infinitesimal pause.

"Bianca," he said softly. "Bianca."

Then he thrust up inside her, deliberately. The orgasm burst through her like fireworks.

"Stephen!" She impaled herself on his engorged cock, shuddering around him. His head rested on her shoulder as he pressed into her, his cock trembling as he filled her with his hot liquid release.

They stayed like that for a long time, clinging to each other as if they never wanted to part. Then he stroked her hair from her face, kissing her cheeks, her eyelids, her mouth.

"Bianca?" he asked quietly.

She swallowed hard.

"Yes," she answered softly. "Bianca."

She wasn't sure why she'd asked him to call her that. But something was happening inside her. She just wasn't sure what . . . not yet.

They'd stayed hidden in his apartment for the past day and night, ordering takeout, not leaving the door of his apartment. They'd made love leisurely, usually walking around his apartment naked, enjoying each other whenever the mood struck—which was often. But Stephen couldn't help but notice that Beth was unhappy.

Was it him, he wondered, with gnawing anxiety? The situation sucked, without question, but he was at least happy that they were together. But as much as she still seemed to enjoy having sex with him, he could still see from the tension of her body and the ghostly frown that was etched beneath her smiling face that something wasn't right. He'd tried dancing around the question, not wanting to make waves, but she'd deflected his questions deftly . . . usually by enticing him to make love again. Not that he was complaining, but he was starting to get a little resentful by the dodge.

She was sitting on his carpet, staring out the window, and the frown was on the surface now.

"All right, that's it," he finally said, sitting cross-legged next to her. "What's going on?"

She looked at him, startled. "What do you mean?"

"Something's upsetting you," he said. "You're obviously not happy here."

"Well, you can't be happy, either," she protested.

He felt a cold stab in his chest. "I'm always happy with you."

She smiled, then leaned up, kissing him.

He pulled away. "Oh no. I'm not getting sidetracked like that again."

"I'm sorry?"

"Baby, I'd make love to you till I was sore," he said, "but not when you're just using it to basically distract me. That's not fair."

She sighed. "I'm not. I mean . . ." She took a deep breath. "I'm sorry that I put you in this position. You're a prisoner in your own home because of me."

He sighed. "I had plenty of vacation time coming. It's not fantastic," he said. "The important part is keeping you safe."

"No," she answered, surprising him. "I can't keep hiding, Stephen. The more I think about it, the more I realize—you were right, back in the Compound. When you said that I was cutting off my life, hiding out. I don't want to do that. What's worse, I don't want to force the man I love to do that, just to stay with me."

"So, what do you want to do?"

She looked at him, her violet eyes huge and liquid.

"I'm Bianca Cordova, of the house of Iko," she said solemnly. "I'm not going to pretend I'm not . . . not anymore."

He smiled, feeling pride warm his heart.

She leaned forward. "And I love you, Stephen Trent," she said. "No matter what my name is, that doesn't change. But my life's about to get a lot more complicated. . . ."

"I can handle it," he said. "Just tell me what I can do to help."

Chapter Sixteen

Beth walked down the marble corridors, her soft-soled shoes making only the slightest hushed echo in the vaulted ceilings. In the years of her absence, she'd forgotten how opulent it was. She'd also forgotten how beautiful the island was. It made her sad, that so much time had gone by.

She wasn't running ever again.

She pushed open the door to the royal bedroom suite, the Queen's private lair. As she'd suspected, she heard the Queen's raised voice.

When Beth's killing had gone wrong, she had gone back to the island to get more money, and to regroup. She expected Beth to try hiding again. She figured she had all the time in the world to find Beth again, and finally kill her, once and for all.

"What do you mean, the damage can't be repaired?" the Queen yelled.

Beth saw her in a mirror. The woman was on the phone, her deformed face contorted with rage. She was so intent on her conversation that she never saw her stepdaughter walking toward her.

"Listen, Weissen, you did this to me. You're supposed to be the best. You'd better goddamn fix it! I look like a hag! A . . . a freak!"

There was a pause.

"I do not have a problem! *You* have the goddamned problem, if you don't fix this!" She slammed the phone down, then threw it at the mirror, shattering it. Then she stood, screaming. "Marisol! Clean this up right now! And get me my—"

She stopped as she took in Beth's presence. She looked surprised. Then she smiled, slowly.

"Well, well," she said, her voice thick with derision. "I see today isn't a total waste. I wouldn't have thought you'd make it so easy for me."

"I'm not afraid of you anymore," Beth said quietly.

"You should be," her stepmother said, advancing on her. "I've waited a long time for this moment."

"So have I," Beth answered. "I just didn't know it."

Beth didn't move. She waited.

"I could have you killed with a snap of my fingers." Her stepmother's eyes blazed.

Beth didn't say anything. She simply snapped.

Her stepmother's misshapen mouth worked silently. When she could finally find words, she screamed. "Guards!"

Within moments, it seemed, red-uniformed guards filed in, obviously used to her beck and call.

Her stepmother pointed at Beth. "Kill her!"

They looked at her stepmother, then at Beth. They pulled out their guns.

Beth turned to them. "You know what to do."

The head guardsman nodded. Then, without a word, they flanked her stepmother.

"What are you doing?" the Queen said, her voice shrill. "I said kill her!"

"She's a daughter of the blood," the guardsman said.

"She's an imposter!"

"She is the image of our Queen. The *real* Queen," he answered. "And she approached the prime minister. She's submitted a blood test. She is Bianca Cordova, true heir of the throne of Iko."

Her stepmother lunged for her, claws out. The guards grabbed her roughly, pinning her arms behind her. Beth simply stood, watching.

"I should have done this years ago," Beth said. "But I was a child, and I was scared. Everyone was scared of you."

"You'll be sorry," her stepmother spat out. "You'll all be sorry! You can't do this to me! *I am the Queen!*"

"You're a traitor," the head guard said sharply. "You've attempted to kill a member of the royal family, which is treason." He paused. "A hanging offense."

Her stepmother went pale. She looked at Beth. "This can't be happening."

"The prime minister is now getting reports that you paid

to have the King killed," he added. "Your subjects aren't afraid of you anymore . . . *Your Majesty*."

His words were ripe with disgust. Beth stared at the woman in shock.

"You had my father killed?"

Her stepmother finally realized the precarious situation she was in. She glanced at the guardsmen.

"I have access to the treasury," she said. "Let me free. I could make it worth your while . . ."

"You've forced enough guards to be your sexual playthings," he said. "I've seen you wreak havoc on my countrymen long enough. You don't have access to anything. And you can't buy your way out of this one."

She growled in fury. Then she looked at Beth, pleading, her voice low.

"You wouldn't let this happen to me," she said. "You're too good a person."

Beth stared at her. "If it were just me that you tried to kill, I'd be happy to let you rot in a cell for the rest of your life."

Her stepmother half smiled.

"But you killed my father," she said. "You killed the King. It's out of my hands now."

Beth turned, hearing her stepmother's curses and howling as the guardsmen dragged her away.

Epilogue

The Princess—now Queen—sank her toes into the pristine white sand of the palace's private beach. The waves that lapped against the shore were impossibly blue, the wind a perfect balmy temperature. She was wearing a small red bikini, her hair up in a ponytail. There was a sumptuous meal laid out on a table, beneath a large hanging umbrella. She reclined on a large white towel, smiling at the setting sun.

"Care for a truffle, Your Majesty?"

She turned to see Stephen, holding a chocolate in his hand. "You know what the tenets of belief say," she joked. "Chocolate is decadent, far too sensual. It leads to lust."

"Damn, I hope so," Stephen said, lying down next to her, his black swim trunks already starting to expand with the length of his erection. He popped the sweet into her mouth. She closed her eyes, moaning as the rich flavor ribboned across

her palate. Then he kissed her, melding his complex masculine flavor with the sweetness of the chocolate. The powerful
combination made her skin tingle with anticipation.

"I'm glad you're back," she whispered, when he pulled away.
"I missed you."

Stephen smiled, his eyes alight. "I told Randall it was the
last undercover story I was going to write," he said. "From
now on, I'll do interviews, and in-depth coverage, but I'm
not going to be that far away from you again."

"You'd think he would've been satisfied with the exclusive
story you got on me," she teased, rolling onto her stomach.
Stephen took another chocolate off of a small plate, placing it
between her lips. She ate it daintily, around a low chuckle.

"That does buy me a lot of leeway," he said, grinning like
a rascal. The exclusive on the "long-dead" Princess of Iko
had been her idea, and it hadn't taken much to convince Stephen to go along with it. At least this way, she knew her story
wouldn't be butchered.

Still, she squirmed. "I don't want to take you away from your
writing," she protested. "I know it's what you love to do."

"And I'll still do it," he said. "I may even finally tackle
the book I've been kicking around, but never had the guts
to go for."

Now, she smiled easily, feeling comforted. "And you think
you'll be okay living here? With me?"

He looked around, gesturing to the magnificent sunset,
the glorious waves, the pristine beach. "Oh, somehow I'll
manage," he drawled.

"That doesn't sound too promising," she joked back. She

propped herself up on one elbow. "Guess I'll have to convince you."

With that, she reached behind her, untying the knot that held up her bikini top. The cloth fell to the towel, leaving her breasts bare.

He licked his lips, then looked around. "Won't someone see us?"

"This is the private palace beach," she said, reaching down and shimmying out of her panties. "I told the servants and guards that no one else is allowed down here until we're back. And don't worry . . . the rain forest makes it impossible for anyone to see anything."

He grinned, slipping out of his trunks. His cock emerged, large and dark with need. "At this point, I don't even care who watches," he said, his eyes alight with wicked promise. "It's been two weeks. I want you, woman."

"Not as much as I want you." She tackled him, and he rolled back on the oversized towel, laughing. His laughter stopped abruptly as she straddled him, her cunt already dripping wet with need. She lowered herself onto his cock, inhaling sharply as he filled her. "God, I missed you, Stephen."

"You'll never have to miss me again," he groaned, lifting his hips, plunging inside her. She tossed her head back, arching her body like a bow handle, swiveling her hips and descending on his hardness. He groaned as she moved swiftly, rising and lowering on his shaft, feeling his blunt cock head press against the inside of her pussy.

She moved faster. His hands held her hips, tugging her to him, burying himself deeper inside her willing softness, and she felt the top of his shaft rubbing against her clit with every downward thrust. She rubbed at it with her fingers, and he watched her, his smile slow and mysterious. She rubbed her breast with her other hand, and he cupped her buttocks, stroking her, clambering for her.

"Beth, Bianca," he said in a rush. "I've wanted you every moment I've been away. I want to feel your pussy clench around me, baby. I want to fuck you till you don't know your own name."

She moaned in response, feeling the orgasm building. "Stephen," she breathed, her hips bucking against him, the feeling growing from her clit and radiating out from her pussy to her breasts, and outward. "Oh, Stephen."

"That's it," he encouraged. "Like that. Just like that. Fuck me, sweetheart. Ride my cock till you come."

Stephen! She felt the orgasm explode around her, and she pounded against him. He groaned, his hips lifting off the towel, lifting them both as he thrust inside her with hard, swift motions. She could feel his ejaculation deep inside her, and her body shuddered around him. The orgasm rolled over her and through her, in continuous waves, until she could barely see or hear. All she could do was feel, and that was mind-blowing.

She collapsed against his chest, curling up against him.

"I guess you showed me," he said, with a soft laugh, stroking her back.

She angled her head up, looking in his face. "Don't mess with me," she said. "I'm the Queen."

"That you are," he admitted. "Although I've got another title for you, if you're interested."

"Really?" She smirked at him. "What title is that?"

His face was serious. "Wife," he whispered.

She swallowed, her heart feeling like it was going to explode with joy.

"What do you say?" he asked, his eyes nervous.

She kissed him, tenderly.

"I love you," she answered. "And I say yes."

"I love you, too," he said, smiling. He went to the table, where he'd hidden a black velvet box. He took out a diamond ring, set in platinum. "Read the inscription."

She glanced in the band. It held only one word.

Forever.

He slipped the ring on her finger. "I promise I'll do everything I can to make you happy."

She smiled.

"Happily ever after," she mused. "I like the sound of that."

CATHY YARDLEY has been entranced by fairy tales since she was three years old. Now, she spends her time weaving those fairy tales into modern retellings that keep the magic, romance, and twisted beauty in entirely contemporary settings and storylines. When not writing, Cathy spends time with her husband and son at home in southern California.

Cathy Yardley